V. CASTRO

MESTIZA BLOOD

This is a **FLAME TREE PRESS** book

FLAME TREE PRESS
6 Melbray Mews, London, SW6 3NS, UK
flametreepress.com

US sales, distribution and warehouse:
Simon & Schuster
simonandschuster.biz

UK distribution and warehouse:
Marston Book Services Ltd
marston.co.uk

Publisher's Note: This is a work of fiction. Names, characters, places, and
incidents are a product of the author's imagination. Locales and public names
are sometimes used for atmospheric purposes. Any resemblance to actual
people, living or dead, or to businesses, companies, events, institutions, or
locales is completely coincidental.

Thanks to the Flame Tree Press team, including:
Taylor Bentley, Frances Bodiam, Federica Ciaravella, Don D'Auria,
Chris Herbert, Josie Karani, Molly Rosevear, Mike Spender,
Cat Taylor, Maria Tissot, Nick Wells, Gillian Whitaker.

The cover is created by Flame Tree Studio with
thanks to Nik Keevil and Shutterstock.com.
The font families used are Avenir and Bembo.

Flame Tree Press is an imprint of Flame Tree Publishing Ltd
flametreepublishing.com

A copy of the CIP data for this book is available from the British Library
and the Library of Congress.

HB ISBN: 978-1-78758-618-5
PB ISBN: 978-1-78758-616-1
ebook ISBN: 978-1-78758-619-2

Printed in the USA by Integrated Books International

V. CASTRO

MESTIZA BLOOD

FLAME TREE PRESS
London & New York

CONTENTS

Dedicated to Jade, Scarlett, Rose and Carrie Castro

NIGHT OF THE LIVING DEAD CHOLA

My tears drip from my mouth and they taste like blood. For years, mud and garbage have weighed down my body to keep me trapped in this wet, dark grave. The tips of my fingers and toes have been nibbled away by fish swimming past my body. They all steal a little morsel of me before scurrying away. I'm surprised there is anything left. As the current fades away, I find myself awake. I am angry. My head throbs from the sound of wailing children above me and the whisper of a goddess below me. I will rise from the depths of the Rio Grande to claim the flesh of those inflicting this pain. I was a ghost in life and still in death, but who knew I would have so much power without a heartbeat or breath?

The Rio Grande is drying up and there is nothing anyone can do about it. Time has increased the temperature in this part of the world, making the border more dangerous from the heat, yet more porous. I've heard all those stories of woe. I hear it in the minds of those who have passed away in these waters. Their memories and dreams float like river grass. Their souls are trapped here with me. Not for long. The Rio Grande is drying up and a solar eclipse is on the horizon.

As the waters become increasingly shallow, the dead have been pushing along the feet of those who wade into our grave. Children and babies are priorities. When they are chased, we claw at the ankles of their pursuers, or hold back the dangers that threaten to pull them below the water. Of course, this has been met with resistance from those above. There is talk of refilling the river, mechanically controlling its currents to be more lethal than ever before. There would be zero survivors. A wall and a river. A modern-day fortress with its moat. The solar eclipse happens tomorrow and tomorrow nothing will ever be the same.

The dark is covering the sky. Two rings appear to become one. They are a vortex of energy that is opening a way for us.

My army of the living dead and I are ready. We rise from the mud, looking like monuments to decay. What is left of our bodies are mere shadows in the darkness. The moon and the sun and the goddess of the dead have gifted life into our flesh. Gifts should not go to waste.

The others are gathering to pound their fists against concrete and canvas walls and rip fences. Their hunger for flesh will be satiated by the ones who try to stop them. Bites will feel like bullets and death that overtakes their bodies will invade like ice. For now, I break from the crowd to find the man who did this to me. My murderer.

He told me I was beautiful, like a dark beauty queen. Just a few beers and a movie was all he wanted. After, when I felt unsteady on my feet even though I wore sneakers and my vision doubled, he wanted to know if he could take a few photos.

I am angry at myself for needing to hear those words from someone other than myself. I am angry that I remain nameless and unsolved, just like those females across the border in Juárez. I'm American. We care about people in America, don't we? After he broke me, used me, made my mascara and eyeliner bleed all over my face, he discarded me like I was nothing. I can still feel part of him inside of me and that is what lets me know where I can find him.

As I follow the trail that leads to my killer, people scream when they see me. Some run, remembering all those films they have watched over the years. A few bullets have pierced my body, but it is not enough to stop me. Before I can get close enough to the shooters, they turn and run the other way. Cowards, too scared of a rotting woman with nothing to lose and a hunger that hurts. They know I will come for them next if someone else hasn't gotten to them first. I ignore the chaos of overturned cars and feasting on flesh that surrounds me to continue on my way.

My memory reminds me his apartment is on the top floor. He is so close now. I can smell his sweat; a stench I will never forget. My belly is hungry for his insides. It stokes my appetite for a bloody stew of caldo. I will devour him the way he devoured me.

With little resistance I push the locked door open. He can hear me. Good. I want him to see me. The sun is back to where it should be high in the sky and there are no remaining shadows to hide any of us.

He stands before me in his underpants. His screams are like a Banda song that tells you the party is about to start. Get to your feet, grab another drink. There is nowhere for him to run as I block the only exit. A puddle of mud and water gathers at my feet as my waterlogged body expunges itself. I'm feeling lighter already. He is stumbling backwards, praying to God for help, but it is a goddess that has brought me here: Mictecacíhuatl, the flayed woman of the underworld and keeper of bones.

His throat is in my hands and I can almost feel myself salivating even though my body is a torn rag of sinew, algae and bone. My teeth are still intact. His blood fills my mouth after his flesh gives in to me so easily. I waste nothing. I sit on the floor to suck every ribbon of muscle from his frame like I would a plate of baby back ribs at a BBQ. I pick little pieces of him from my teeth, like corn on the cob. His skull makes the sound of a coconut falling to the ground as I open it to slurp my dessert.

The bones are left for the queen to collect and use as bricks for her underworld kingdom. I hope she uses them to cobble a road. My meal has left me sluggish. I lie down to sleep, just for a moment, and maybe dream of all the things I didn't get to do in life.

It is night again. The moonlight is the only source of light. As I move to raise myself from the floor, I look at my hands, my body. My flesh has been made whole again. My stomach churns with excitement and meat. I jump to my feet and run to the bathroom. I touch my skin, which looks as if I have just stepped out of the shower. Beneath the mirror, there is makeup. The asshole has a lady. I find this disturbing. He didn't seem like one for a relationship. The red Maybelline pencil feels good in my hands. I hope I haven't forgotten how to use it. My eyebrows need filling, eyes need lining. Like two friends that have been apart but come back together as if no time has passed, I create a perfect stroke at the corner of my eyes. The dark shade of red, bordering on brown, lipstick with matching lip liner suits my skin color. A quick brush through my hair leaves it long and smooth as it falls over my shoulders. I part it right in the middle to accentuate my high cheek bones and round face. This ritual reminds me how I would sneak clothes and lipstick in my backpack before school to change into later because my mom didn't want me looking like trouble. I wonder where she is now. Speaking of clothes, I am nude.

If there is makeup there has to be clothing. I go through the chest of drawers and find panties and a tank top. In the closet there are jeans that are too long and slightly baggy. No problem. I take a belt and cinch them in at the waist. There is a pile of women's shoes in different sizes. This is odd. Beneath this tower of leather, I find a box of phones, jewelry, driver's licenses, including mine. Suddenly I feel sick. I want to vomit, and I do. The thought of this beast inside of me fills me with anger and hate. I vomit more, until every scrap of him is out of me. I throw open the closet to pull everything out. My old Nike Cortezes are in the corner. I know they are mine because there is blue ink with my initials on the back. I did that. There is also my mini backpack, inside of which is a beat-up copy of *The House on Mango Street* by Sandra Cisneros.

I wipe the remnants of vomit from my mouth and return to the bathroom to reapply my lipstick. I wonder who wore these clothes and makeup before me. Perhaps they will have a second chance as I did. A rumble inside of me alerts me that I am hungry again. Tonight, I will go out and find another meal to satisfy my appetite. I take everything I can find of value, including car keys.

A TV in the next apartment is on loudly. I hear a news alert. The Rio Grande has dried up and there is nothing the army or police or politicians can do about it. The bodies of the dead and ghosts have returned as well. People are also claiming their dead relatives are returning as if they had never died at all, except for a new appetite. "God help us all," the newsreader concludes, "because it looks like they might just take over."

THE DEMON IN MY EYE

I woke up this morning wanting to die. I told myself it's just the demon in my eye, a little bug stuck inside my pupil. It often tells me to surrender to its call. Hell is so much easier to endure than here. I imagine there is a sense of peace in oblivion. No noise, no doubt, no heartache. Part of me believes the voice. All I would have to do is fly straight into a brick wall and allow my eyes to close after I hear the sound of my skull cracking open. Brain huevos rancheros for the flesh-eating pigeons as large as vultures. Haven't made a single level-headed decision in my life. It's a life I'm destined to endure until the end of days, I'm afraid.

The demon in my eye is a little bug I can't remove to relieve myself of this craven thirst that devours everything and instructs me to kill anyone who does me wrong, sometimes right, and corrupts anything that is good that might come my way. But it has kept me alive in a time when survival is the only thing that matters. Well, that and who you roll with.

A cold body bumps next to me, a soft moan. Christ, he's barely alive. I roll out of bed, smelling of my own pussy and dried cum, knowing there is only one way to salvage this situation. I have ten missed calls on my watch blinking red on the bedside table next to an empty bottle of rum. I grab my companion's white-collared shirt crumpled on the floor and step into the motel hallway. I need to find the kitchen and housekeeping storage room fast, both typically in the basement these days. Everyone is still asleep as I quickly rush past the quiet rooms to the stairwell down four levels. Bingo. In the basement I find housekeeping. I grab four plastic laundry bags with drawstrings. Next, time to hit up the kitchen. I hear voices, but one look at me and they will do exactly as they are told.

"Bro, she still won't let me hit it. Says she scared of catching something. I told her I'd wrap it up with a body bag if it'll—" The squat muscly guy stops his story and looks at me with wide eyes trembling with fear. A silver ladle quakes in his hand.

"I want all these bags filled with ice. Now."

The two kitchen staff approach me with caution before they snatch the bags from my outstretched hand and fumble awkwardly to do as ordered. I spot an insulated box used for cold storage. Perfect.

"Put the bags in that box." They both nod and move faster while keeping an eye on me in their peripheral vision.

"Thanks. And tell your chick she has nothing to worry about. She won't catch nothing out there. Maybe a case of crabs from you. The vaccine is legit. We made sure of that."

They remain silent and nod with their jaws hanging open as I dash out and back to the room as fast as I got down. My plaything's pulse is about to give out. Even if I wanted to, I couldn't save him. We sucked and fucked so hard, but that's what you get when you fuck with a woman like me. He took so much milk last night he won't feel this. I told him to slow down. They never listen. Nobody listens to women.

I take out my compact surgical kit. I've got minutes to do this, but I've become so good I should be rolling with the Doctors. One last breath leaves his mouth. With gloved hands I spray the inside of the ice bags and his entire body with antiseptic mist. I stick his belly with a cauterizing scalpel, careful not to damage anything below his layer of fat. A shame, because he was a great fuck, eager to please me. He slurped all the milk secreted from between my legs and tits until my thighs shook.

*　　*　　*

I toss my bloody gloves on the sheet when I'm finished. The Doctors will be happy to get these scraps for the weird but important work they do. Time to get dressed. I pull on my denim jacket with large slits beneath the sleeves to accommodate my anatomy. Everything I own must be custom made. Then it's time to head to the Pawn N Thrift, owned by my old friend Larv. He is the absolute best in the black market of organ dealing.

From the glass front door of the shop I can see Larv in the back inspecting something. A little bell jingles as I walk in. Square plastic bags filled with blood, plasma, eyeballs and milk hang with their tails trailing like freakish jellyfish within the temperature-controlled cases. The bags glow like jewels and the eyes look like Fabergé eggs with the soft lighting behind them. Larv puts an antique drone down.

"Hey, Valencia. You got something good for me?"

I place the box on the counter and open it. "Yeah, liver, lungs, kidneys and a heart that'll only be good for the arteries."

"A heart? I thought you Mexicans just love the heart?" I can smell his eggy breath as he chuckles.

"Now *you* tell me something good. What can you give me?"

"How 'bout you come back here and suck me off. Always wanted to get off with a woman like—"

"You really want me to do that? I'll chomp that shit off like a handful of potato chips. Might sound the same too." I show him my stained teeth with a wide grin to reinforce the message. I can still taste the residual copper of blood in my mouth. My face must look extra menacing.

"All right, no need to be vulgar." He smiles and shows me the slimy gold grill in his mouth. His muscled chest quakes beneath a tight black t-shirt. His pecs are almost as big as my tits.

"You want trade or coin?"

"I need coin. Same account."

He slides a chart in front of me and points out a number. It's the new price list. The Bankers raised their cut for using coin and the Doctors obviously agreed. Damn. I guess lasting peace has a price too.

"Good for me."

"All right. Don't go breaking any necks or hearts today. And bring that wicked ass around here more often. I keep getting requests for your milk."

I turn on my heels and give him the middle finger before flipping my hair. "Adios, Larvae baby."

The dawn is just breaking as I walk out. I pull up my mask to filter out the pollutants in the air. For a while it was better, but now we've returned to the old ways; the city buildings are blackened with soot and garbage goes uncollected for weeks at a time. I crouch before leaping into the air in flight.

The brown downy hairs on my neck and spine catch the breeze as I fly above the city lights, above the sorrow we have all become. I'm heading back to our camp south of the river now named the River Styx for the makeshift morgues that floated when there was no longer any room for all the dead in the cities. No room to bury them and not even time to burn them in mass graves. Those bodies eventually floated into the ocean never to be seen again. None of the other gangs dares cross the river unless invited. We made sure of that after the last turf war.

It's a short flight to the landing path just outside the barricaded warehouse that used to house helicopters for rich folks. Fuck. Tony is outside, probably waiting for me. I land softly, my thin bat wings folding like an accordion back into the soft openings from under my armpits to my wrists via the slits in my jacket.

"You didn't come back last night." He steps close and sniffs my skin. "And you weren't alone."

"None of your business, Tony. I told you I'm not a one-man kind of woman. Plus, I got this." I pull out the eye from the light bag around my waist to show him. "My ticket into Johnson Labs."

"There really isn't anything you won't do to get what you want."

"Nope. Including fucking someone. He was good too."

There is enough morning light for me to see the red in his cheeks and the scowl on his face, the billows of black smoke from the morning fires rising in the air as toxic as this man's kiss. His eyes just as black as the grime we sneeze from our noses.

"You're a fucking slut tease. You know that?"

"Go back to the dog pound. Just because there's a truce doesn't mean there isn't bad blood between us. And that kind of talk is why I don't fuck with you."

"You'll be back when you figure out you can't get better," I hear him shout as I walk away.

I turn around because I can't resist putting a final nail in this love-gone-wrong coffin. "You're right, I will be back. I'll be back when I come to drain you of your blood and sell your organs to Larv."

I leave him, feeling flush. It took a long time for me to tell him that, considering I'm the most hardheaded and desperate to be loved individual I know. But as soon as I get it, I don't want it anymore.

I walk through the main door of the warehouse to see Peggy standing there wringing her pink-and-brown-spotted hands, absently watching a group of teens sorting through clothing.

"Hey, Peggy. Your snout's a little wet. You been snorting that slop again?"

She huffs from her large nostrils and touches her round cheeks. "Huh? No. You need to hurry. Tina got news the Evangelicals are gonna make another move, possibly try to start another war between the gangs so they can push us out. You know what they would do to us?"

Fucking Evangelicals. I rush past her to the office in the back. The rest of the warehouse is used for sorting goods either stolen, found outside of the cities, or in abandoned gated communities stockpiled with shit the dead left behind.

When I enter the office, Tina glances up from her tablet with her lizard-like eyes, looking worried and pissed off.

"I might have sent Tony to find you if you didn't show up by noon. It's bad." She rolls out an old map of the city on the conference room table we took from the looting of city hall. "The Hazmats have moved to the north border of the river and the Dogs resettled in the slaughter district. But we have word from one of the Hazmats the Evangelicals and Skinheads have joined forces with Uptown under you know who."

"Lemme guess, our old friend Karen." Fucking Karen Hughs, the long-suffering and sad widow of Eric Hughs.

Tina nods. "She'll be hosting a small meeting with both of the other gangs trying to take us down with promises of turf and our bodies. The Doctors said they're neutral as before and they'll only offer medical assistance. But this is our chance. Who knows when we'll have three of the worst gang leaders in one room? They were the only ones who prevented lasting peace under Captain."

No way would Karen make a slave of me or anyone. "What you want from me?"

"I want you to infect them. We know for a fact they haven't been vaccinated. Plus, the brownstone block is protected to the teeth. But I think if the low-level goons see their leaders gone, they might just run like the cowards they are, especially considering half of them are paid. No real loyalty there. You're the only one who can approach from a different angle, the sky. They probably don't think any of you exist anymore. I'm one of the four Komodo dragons left and we're slow as hell on two legs. If you needed brawn, I'd be your woman."

"Not gonna do it. I don't want to risk any part of my DNA getting out. We have more and more orphans finding their way here. What if my blood's mutated? Last night I got a free ticket

into Johnson Labs to test myself. I won't infect them, but I will
kill them for the sake of everyone. It will be my pleasure to rid
the city of Karen Hughs."

"So it's a yes for getting this done?" Tina is just like me and
takes 'no' as a sign there's another way. Our collective female
rage has created a sort of magnetic field that keeps us safe enough.
And she can snap bones in seconds with her bite. "This happens
tonight. We can't waste any time with this. She is one tricky cunt
moving place to place. I think she's only settling uptown because
she thinks she can take over the entire city if she pays enough
goons. Probably wants her old pad back too."

"Consider it done. If I die, please give my shit to Peggy. She is
one sappy sow. What about retaliation? Any plan for that?"

Tina rolls up the map, slumps into her office chair and grabs a
small mouse from an aquarium. She swallows it whole. "Same as
always. Give Peggy the order on your way out."

I walk out of the office to Peggy, who's still snorting in
obvious agitation. I place a hand on her shoulder. "Hey. Don't
worry. Tonight you have an important job. I need you to take all
the orphans to the boats. Read them stories, play games, but keep
them calm and safe. Don't think about anything else. If things go
bad, you do as we practiced."

"What about you? What are you two planning?"

"Don't think about me twice. I don't matter. Those orphans,
got it?"

She looks at me with watery eyes. I know there would be
no stopping the hug, so I allow her to squeeze me, her snout
burrowing in the side of my neck. "Be careful," she whispers.

I walk away to sit by the river, wanting to be alone. Not even
a year ago Karen and her husband killed the Captain. He was part
of our crew trying to unify the gangs to work together instead
of squabbling over blocks in a city now resembling something
out of a story set during twentieth-century industrialization, but

with more graffiti. Nothing worked; people starved on the streets, disease ravaged the population, leaving only shitty folks like me to do whatever it took to survive. I've had to sell my body, its precious secretions. I've also sold body parts because flesh is currency that exists as long as we exist. Anything and everything is for sale.

We're the Animals, freakish and mostly ruthless.

The Captain thought we could all get along, no matter what our differences. Optimistic bastard got himself killed. Right before our eyes in a packed stadium, He exploded into a million pieces when he stepped up to the podium to declare a truce between the rival gangs and free passes through turf to create some semblance of civilization, like it ever existed. The only one against unification was Karen Hughs and her pharmaceutical CEO husband. They sowed dissent by spreading rumors and preying on the fears of the Evangelicals and Skinheads. Captain was the closest chance we got to living together without our pettiness getting in the way.

I sit there thinking about the past until the sun sets, my demon itching to get out and toss my ass into the river. Its hiss begins like steam escaping a pipe until the temperature and pressure climbs and my mind is awash with anger and thoughts of blood.

There isn't a single breeze or gust of wind tonight to propel me faster. I have to fly hard across the city with only patches of electricity working. No airplanes anymore either. Thankfully I had the foresight to ditch my boots, exposing my clawed feet. I wear only a thin ribbed tank top cut just under the breasts and black tear-resistant leggings. My surgical kit is strapped to my thigh and a single blade is strapped to my ankle, with the rest of me exposed to whatever weapons they might have, but I couldn't fly quick enough with anything else on.

I land softly on top of the brownstone that back in the twenty-first century probably cost a few million. Karen and her crew have taken an entire block overlooking a once grand park. It needs a good clear-out. The Captain had dreams of restoring it, perhaps as a neutral zone market. My demon screeches for organ meat when I think of our big plans taken in seconds. The Evangelicals and Skinheads had joined Karen's ranks, slowly moving in. The Skinheads loved the chaos as much as the Evangelicals. This end-of-world scenario fit in nicely with their fucked-up version of reality and prophecy.

I creep to the edge of the roof and peer towards the fire escape. Nobody there, but the ground has at least twenty-five armed bodies patrolling, mostly talking amongst themselves instead of looking vigilant. I climb down, hoping one of the windows will be open on a hot night like this, with not enough consistent power for air con. The city is a perpetual cloud of pollution and heat. The rain gives us some relief unless it comes down as acid.

One of the windows further down appears open, but shit, an ugly motherfucker with his back turned guards the room. He's a skinhead with a cross tattoo that begins at the base of his neck and ends on the back of his head, where the cross turns into a swastika. What a fucking moron if there ever was one. I can't wait to kill him where he stands. I can feel myself salivating, my hunger growing and the milk inside of me churning.

With one swift movement I dart inside, unhinge my jaw and clamp onto the back of his neck before he can react. I sever his spine with one bite. Blood floods my mouth and sprays my face as I rip out the spinal column. I can feel his blood leaching into my gums and eyes. My body readily absorbs it with orgasmic high voltage. I catch him before he can fall and make noise. Shame. Could have got good money for his organs. I don't bother with his weapon because it will only make noise and outside the brownstone there are more guards than I can handle alone. I slide him into the closet. I can't hear anyone in the hallway but there are voices in another room. I walk quietly so I can make out what they're saying.

"Praise Jesus we are here today. Together we will wipe out those godforsaken things, so vile they could only be from Satan in this End of Days."

Fucking Evangelical John. I know him from his radio blasts trying to create a new flock of those 'left behind'. Motherfucker organized his gang from prison where he served time for stealing millions from his church and promising a miracle cure for all the 'foreign viruses sneaking across the borders'. Well, one riot later, when shit got really bad in the prisons, he became a regular Jim Jones. He claimed to be a living miracle. Humans can be so fucking dumb when scared.

"Yes," Karen Hughs says, "my dearest husband built his fortune to help those that help themselves. When this is all over, I will allow both of your people to decide what to do with the gangs that don't fall in line. I care little for the Animals. I do care about the legacy my husband had in mind. A new way of leading."

"Yes, repent and accept Jesus or death," Evangelical John says in his fake pious tone.

"I don't think any of them are pure. Tainted blood should never mix. Let them rebuild what we lost. Show them who the real master is in a new confederacy." That has to be a Skinhead. I don't know much about them except they keep to themselves in one ideological hateful circle jerk with the morals of a virus.

Suddenly I want to infect them all, let them writhe on the floor and transform or die a horrible death as their body rejects what's inside my bat DNA, which was harmless until some human fuck from Johnson Labs decided to fuck with me. Tubes and needles, experiment after experiment after they took me off the streets on my way home from the library where I worked. Now all those lab coats are dead, but their research is still very much alive and locked in Johnson Labs. How can I ever be free without the freedom to be who I was born to be? Stripped and mutated to be something more palatable but made into a nightmare. And once the nightmare got loose, it was they who lost.

The demon in my eye is begging to be let out. To kill and destroy. That's why I'm here, not to get caught or killed. As much as I couldn't care less if I live or die, I can't die until these putrid sacks of flesh are gone.

I slide my back down the wall and ball my fists. The demon is stronger, telling me what a shitbag I am, and I'm bound to fuck it up. I slap myself hard, the sharp tips of my nails catching the flesh on my cheek. I would let myself fall into a puddle of tears if any of the moisture in my body could be spared. Only the milk matters. The milk that's a side effect of my transformation.

I move to my hands and knees and crawl on the floor with my tongue hanging out. Wings want to splay so they might see me in my full animal glory. Evangelical John sees me first.

"God in heaven, how did that get in here? Jezebel from hell! Jesus, strike this demon vermin down now! I command you!"

I know he's the least dangerous, so I turn my attention to the Skinheads' leader, who has to be in his forties but has a solid build I can see though his tight golfing shirt and jeans. He pulls out a sawed-off shotgun from the side of his leg and points the barrel at me.

"No, don't!" screams Karen. "If she explodes and blood gets everywhere, we're goners. It'll release what's inside of her. I thought all of her kind were dead. I personally saw to their termination when my husband and I ran Johnson Labs." Her tone drips of smug satisfaction. Her face is shiny and tight from her last face lift. Her yellowed pearls and cardigan with holes look like something she stole from a corpse. Some people just don't know how to move on.

I can see the Skinhead wants to do it. The hate in his mind is a demon he can't control either because it's so deep inside now. It makes his hand tremble and a vein next to his right eye twitch. I use this to my advantage.

I scramble across the floor, straight for his nuts, to bite and pull. Blood gushes from the open space between his legs. He screams and drops the shotgun. His body falls to the floor, where he bleeds out. Evangelical John, a coward like all his kind, runs for the door. I zip through the air and land on his back. I stick two fingers into his nostrils and pull until his flesh rips from his skull. I turn around to find Karen with her back against the wall, watching the murder unfold.

"Ryan!" she shouts into the bracelet on her wrist.

With a single movement I toss the blade in her direction. It grazes her neck. She screams out and places a hand on the wound to stop the bleeding. Her pearls and cardigan are soaked in crimson.

You missed, you asshole. You're finally gonna die, the demon says to me.

Karen is losing the color in her face fast. "If I didn't hate your kind so much, I'd say you're pretty majestic. Now don't do this. Let's make a deal. What if I said I have someone inside the Doctors working on a cure?"

I hear stomping footfalls on stairs. Someone, probably Ryan, has bolted from downstairs and I'm between Karen and this guy, who is staring at me in disbelief. Well, at least my tits. Milky white streaks my abdomen and soaks through my tank top.

"You can either stop this now and be an informant," Karen says, "or Ryan will tranquilize your ass and we will do things to you that are worse than anything you can imagine. You'll be a milk pump pumping coin into my pocket from the highest bidders. Maybe I'll give you to the Skinheads for their pleasure or the Evangelicals to purify you with fire."

Ryan reminded me of Tony. I lift my top. "Hey, Ryan. How would you like a taste?" The milk leaking from my body is like the milk of the poppy, sweet and addictive. I think this might have happened because the lab coats kept me drugged up for so long. Won't know for certain until I get my hands on those files. Ryan licks his lips, and his eyes dart between me and Karen.

"Don't you fucking dare." She lifts her wrist to call backup.

Before she has a chance, Ryan points his weapon and shoots her between the eyes. He lowers his tranquilizer and I open my arms to take him to my bosom and let him fall into my brown wings. The pearly liquid drips with a honey-like viscosity and he hungrily drinks. I tenderly brush away the hair from his brow. He can't be more than twenty, most probably grew up on the streets.

"You know there's a price to pay for this. Some die and others change. You'll either find your way to us or strike out beyond the city."

He looks up with desperate and sad eyes like all the others, just wanting something to suckle to ease the pain of this shitty life we brought upon ourselves. He falls into a deep sleep. I look around at the carnage and see nothing but coin.

But first things first.

⋆   ⋆   ⋆

"You're back. That was quick. You have some of your sweet leche for me?"

"Nope. Even better." I grab the trash bag filled with plastic tubs of organs. "Three hearts. Evangelical, Skinhead and Karen, plus all of their livers and kidneys."

He looks hungrily at the bags before leaning back in his chair. "Yo, Worm. Come and get this stuff. I'm eating."

A scrawny brown boy with a feathery adolescent moustache over his top lip and a shaved head enters from the back. "All right, Dad. I need to call the Doctors for the rest?"

Larv looks at me with a half smile. "This from what went down at the brownstones? I've been getting alert after alert."

"Let's just say don't call the Doctors. That place will be crawling with scum soon trying to find a way to take over. We need to stay in good with the only neutral group."

"I'll give you double what you got last time if you bring some of your leche."

"No can do. It's about to get nasty. Better board up the front and keep Worm off the streets. They'll be looking for any brown body or animal to capture."

"Okay. Triple still for the heads up. Take care of yourself, Valencia."

I take flight just as the dawn breaks to head back to the warehouse. Tina is waiting with our small board of directors, I guess you could call us. She and the five others clap as I land.

Tina hands me a bottle of homemade mezcal mixed with blood. "I can't believe you tossed their heads out the window with notes attached. You did it."

"I did. Got some coin out of it too for our organization. But I'm exhausted. I'm going to sleep for a few hours."

"A few hours? Why not for a few days?"

"I'm heading to Johnson Labs tonight. Got some files to steal and I want to test my blood."

"Well, you better come get me first. I owe you one. I'm so busy with trying to revive Captain's work I haven't had a good bone crushing in a while. Could be fun to get in a scrap, sharpen my nails."

"Damn straight."

"Hey. You think you can really find something to cure you of that voice in your head? 'The demon' you call it? You really want to change what you are?"

I shrug and shake my head. I'll only take a few more swigs of the booze because I want to be fresh for tonight. It's a ten-minute stroll to the decrepit riverside condos we took over about five years ago. Captain made sure we had running water and electricity three times a week. All the orphans live in the basement for their safety. It's where I sleep if I'm not in a motel or hotel doing what I do best. My body feels sluggish and drained the longer I walk. Always does when I release milk like that. I should shower but I can't find the energy. The demon in my eye tells me I'm a dirty thing anyway. No need to clean myself because what good would it do? Neither sin, skin, nor nature can be washed away. I close my eyes and dream of azure cenotes and dark caves of Mexico. I am a bat after all. This city was never my home.

DONKEY LADY BRIDGE

July 1

People like to call it Donkey Lady Bridge. Kids and drunk teens dare each other to run across while making donkey sounds, but nothing has ever happened to them. By the corner of the bridge you can see remnants of black wax and chalk marks where wannabe Satanists go to perform seances. Then there are others minding their own business, who swear there is a malevolent presence. A real estate agent charged with auctioning the land changed offices so she would never have to venture in that part of town again. It was always the ones who weren't looking for the Donkey Lady who got her attention. I didn't believe any of it. I drove across that bridge so many times without so much as a glare across my windshield.

Everyone who lives around here has a different story about who Diana, the Donkey Lady, is or was. The story I heard, and the version that frightens me the most, is that she was the victim of a Santería ritual gone wrong, a curandera caught in something beyond her control as she sought revenge against her abusive partner. The house where it was supposed to have happened is a burnt ruin nestled amongst the trees and bushes that have been left to grow wild. This notoriously 'haunted' spot is just beyond the bridge. There is a permanent faded 'For Sale' sign half tipped over stuck deep into the ground.

Now, I wear a cross around my neck. I've read every book in the library about Santería, even trying to convince a practitioner to tell me its secrets. However, I was met with suspicion and a slammed door in my face. This audio diary is to keep track of my investigation. I also want there to be some record of what I am doing in case anything should happen to me. Here goes.

What I wouldn't give to take back that night three weeks ago when I decided to walk across that bridge. The ladies and I were out for drinks. It was one of those nights where we all just wanted to have a good bitch fest about work, men, the never-ending exhaustion of adulting, and misbehaving kids. That night, we were going to drink our fun until double vision took over and at least one of us would text an ex, followed by tearful regret. I knew all of this, yet I still drove to the bar directly after work, even though it wasn't that far from my condo. Sometimes that Friday feeling is the only thing to propel you forward when the rest of the week is nothing short of a shit show.

We got hammered on pitchers of margaritas. When Nadine ordered a round of tequila shots, I could feel my stomach churn from the smell. I needed food; greasy, stodgy, intestine-rotting, processed junk. That unsteady, mind-spinning feeling of slowly drowning in murky water began to take over. In my drunken state I walked out of the bar and into the freshness of the night. The darkness was speckled with the little backsides of fireflies and insects sang their night hymns. The warmth of the Texas summer evening enveloped my body. I wanted to go home. Of course, I couldn't drive in my state of inebriation.

My car was safe enough overnight in this quiet part of town. An oversized t-shirt and the thought of UberEats delivery called to me a lot louder than the tone-deaf karaoke going on inside. I began to walk home, not noticing when I was across the bridge. A rustle in the brush alerted me to my location. Instinctively, I took out my phone while pretending to talk loudly to someone as I walked. My other hand fumbled for a small bottle of pepper spray inside my handbag. Nothing is more sobering than fear.

The rustling persisted. Maybe this was just some weirdo

wanting to jerk off in front of me or a bunch of kids playing a prank. Nice try, assholes. My fear was turning to annoyance.

Then I heard it. It was a hoarse, strangled cry of despair, pain and hate. It was a sound that felt like the thorax of hell decided to open and bestow upon humanity its horrible song.

I turned my head towards the trees, flipped on my phone's flashlight app and directed it to whatever was making that noise while moving closer to the sound. I've always hated people in horror films who felt the need to investigate instead of run. Now, I was one of those idiots.

At first, I didn't know what I was seeing. The silhouette was roughly the size of a large dog sitting upright. The face was undiscernible as matted hair clung from the scalp, clotted with what looked like mud and blood. Its hands and feet resembled hooves as its fingers and toes appeared split in the middle, fused three by two by melted skin. As it lifted its head, I could see two breasts hanging low like masses of stretched misshapen dough. It was a woman. I stared, trying to understand what was before my eyes. She stared right back at me. My mouth opened to scream but no sound escaped. I turned to run. Behind me I could hear twigs and fallen leaves underfoot of the woman in the trees. However, it wasn't the sound of two feet. She was practically galloping.

Pain seared behind my knees as she drove her head into my legs. I was now eating dirt as I lay flat on my stomach. Miraculously my hand still clutched my phone. There was no one to call who could get to me in time, but perhaps I could try to fling it at her face. Before I followed through with the assault, a curtain of black tangled hair appeared in my peripheral vision.

Slowly I turned my head to see what I might be up against. She opened a large inhuman mouth to let out another strained, guttural cry, like a donkey. I tried to still my quivering body as she brought her elongated countenance next to mine. The bones in her face looked like they had been broken multiple times and set back improperly. Her nose, wet with snot, sniffed around my face. Strings of saliva dribbled from open lips, revealing teeth that resembled a forgotten cemetery. They were a cluttered collection of tombstones on top of each other, chipped away with rot. A fog of stinking breath puffed against my forehead. I could feel margarita mix and bar nuts scrambling from the pit of my stomach to my throat. My bladder tightened then wanted to relieve itself of its fright. I couldn't look into her eyes. They would surely bore into my memory and I would never forget this sight if I escaped. Instead I stared at the mottled keloid skin that made up her front hooves where hands should be. Neglected nails were thick, yellowed, jagged shards. One kick would tear right through me.

My eyes traveled further up without any control, as if invisible marionette strings pulled at my pupils. Something wanted me to look into her eyes. Across her chest a thick welt cast an angry red mark of what could have only been a chain and crucifix, the burns so deep I could imagine the gold melted directly into her skin and the bones of her sternum.

I felt dizzy with fear, thinking this would be the end of me, as my eyes were still moving to meet hers. They were black, vast, empty wells of pain and sorrow. Tears streamed from the corners. Then she screeched again with an evil donkey call. This gave me just the amount of time to get a good swipe with my large Samsung phone across her head.

I scrambled to my feet, losing a shoe in the process, and ran as fast as I could. I couldn't hear anything besides the blood pumping between my ears. It wasn't until I got home that I realized the bottom of my left foot was torn to ribbons from running barefoot. A bloody footprint trailed through the house into the bathroom.

As I looked into the bathroom mirror, there she was staring back at me with that misshapen elongated face and wet nose. Her black eyes became wider as she opened her mouth to scream her lonely lamentation.

I went to call out for my husband but all that escaped was a hoarse donkey cry. I couldn't form words, only a name echoing in my mind: "Diana."

"Jackie! Jackie! Stop screaming! What happened to you?" I emerged from this weird vision to my husband, Miguel, shaking me by my arms. I melted into his body and began to sob. Miguel automatically assumed the worst by the look of me. When I finally told him the story, I could tell he was trying to stifle laughter.

"Look, you just had too much to drink with the girls. Have you told them you're all right?"

I shook my head. "Yeah, I had a few missed texts. But by the look of their Instagram stories they didn't miss me much."

Miguel continued to clean my foot as I sat on the toilet. My ravenous appetite had disappeared. Later, I didn't want to close my eyes from the fear she would appear again, so I sat in bed, searching for any information I could on the property just beyond the bridge.

Before going to bed I discovered I must have dropped my bag when I fell. We would have to go back tomorrow. No way did I want to go through the hassle of calling my bank and credit cards – donkey lady or no donkey lady. I'm pretty sure it would be there. I also needed to know she existed, and that I didn't imagine any of this.

After lunch, my Miguel and I went to the bridge. I brought flowers, votive candles sprinkled with blood from my wounded foot and fruit to leave at the spot where she attacked me. I knew she had to be real. It was curious she hadn't followed me, and when I thought about it, she didn't really hurt me when she could have. There was something that didn't feel right or add up. Miguel was trying to be nice but still managed to roll his eyes when he saw my little offering in hand.

We walked the area, trying to find where I had been the previous night. I found my fallen ballet flat. I hoped to find anything else that might prove to my husband she was real, and I wasn't just a hot mess caught in my own booze-fueled nightmare.

No trace of anything, except the marks on my body that could be explained as self-inflicted from the fall. Without realizing where I was going, I found myself in the line of trees where I first saw her. I continued through the trees, hoping to come across evidence of her existence.

There it was: the burned residence people claimed was that of the Donkey Lady, Diana. That name played over and over like a stalled tape recorder. I whispered her name as I laid down my offering. In the distance I could hear Miguel shouting that he found my bag. He would want to leave soon. I did a quick scan of what was left of the property. Not so much as a pile of dung or food wrappers. Did I really think a woman was living in these woods for years undetected? Did I really believe in a spirit world? I returned to our car unafraid, with a determination to find some answers.

July 10

She won't leave my mind. Since the day I left my first offering, I've been going back to the property to leave offerings after work. Whenever I'd return on my way to work the following day, it would be gone. Miguel says it's a homeless person or animals, but I don't think so. I also left clothes. They were gone too, except in their place I found an old VHS tape partly covered in a dried white substance.

That was the first clue that might lead to something, because I'd found no news stories or a shred of evidence to tell me what might have happened there. The real estate agent who was meant to auction the property refused to speak to me about the details of ownership. The new agent said the exact same thing, as the property belongs to the bank.

I have to find a VHS player as soon as possible because some things are not meant to be mysteries.

July 12

I found a VHS player, but it seems the video is damaged. Why would someone leave it if I wasn't supposed to see what was on it? So, I did a little research and found a guy to try to restore the tape. We'll meet tomorrow at lunch. Fingers crossed, prayers to Santa Muerte, La Virgen, and anything else that wants to pitch in and lend a hand.

July 13
It's Friday the 13th and I'm scared to watch the video. The guy who repaired the VHS said if I don't go to the police, he will. He also told me to never reach out to him again should I find any other media. Wish me luck, as I need to watch this before Miguel comes home.

Later
My God. I feel my very soul has been sucked from my body. I have never seen anything as horrific as what was on the VHS tape. There was a woman, a crowd of people, if you can call them people. What she endured. I...I can't. And that thing. I can't even begin to describe it or how I can go on with my faith. Maybe I need more faith to understand what I just saw. Can I trust my eyes?

I've made a copy of the tape on DVD and sent it to the police anonymously along with the original VHS tape. Maybe their forensics can do something more to find her murderers or family who may be looking for her.

Tomorrow is my birthday. Everyone making a big deal about it except me. All I can think about is the woman on the tape. May Miguel and my family forgive me. I'm going to that bridge tomorrow.

[*The tape ends at this point.*]

The aroma in the air reminds me of a compost pile. It's a sick smell that doesn't leave your nose easily. There is also a scent of singed meat lingering in the air. It conjures the image of Diana's fused hands and feet. The video. I suddenly feel as if I am not alone. There is the sound of breaking twigs in front of me. Through the clearing I see her. That ragged grease stain of hair, the torn, muddied dress, the one she wore the night she attacked me. We stare at each other, neither of us moving. I have brought food in a bag in case she is flesh and blood. I hope that she is real because if she is at least I can help her. Perhaps she has family somewhere. Those evil things in the video must be punished. I want to see them punished.

My anger is greater than my fear, which causes my feet to move. She remains still, looking at me with her wet eyes and nose. Her tongue slides over rotted teeth and bulbous lips. I get close enough to smell her. She has to be real. My hand reaches for the apple slices in my bag. She moves her face closer and cocks her head. Before I can try to touch her, she turns and walks into the woods. I do not move until she turns back to me as if to say, "Why aren't you following?" I begin to walk in her direction. I don't know these woods. In fact, I think we have moved from the unsold property to somewhere else, as I have to climb over a decaying wood fence.

We walk for what seems like an hour, completely shaded underneath trees, bringing the temperature down. I feel the chill as I continue to trail behind what might or might not be flesh. We reach a small clearing with nothing except six dirt mounds and an open pit. I went looking for evil and I have found it.

The stench takes me back to my childhood when I found my auntie's dog, Petunia, devouring her puppies. The smell of rotting meat sizzling under the sun clung to the grass for days. The dog sat there with her sad eyes, gnawing on the discarded bones, viscera strewn across the yard. I screamed and ran into the house to vomit. That smell never left my senses and today it is here. I grab my phone and begin to dial 911. It's busy. I continue to dial with no answer. Diana sits perched above what I assume is an open grave. I don't want to look but I feel compelled to see if it is her body or another in the pit. As I walk towards the open earth, I feel like I will see myself in that grave.

I look into the hole. There is nothing there until I feel myself falling forward. My face is in the dirt. Worms are squirming beneath my fingers. Mud clings to my lips. I turn to the opening of the pit to see her looking down at me. There are tears in her eyes. She screams out an agonizing donkey call before using her fused feet and hands to push dirt and debris over my body. I'm trying to climb out, but I can't because the earth is too soft. How the hell did this hole get so big? It looks like someone was using it to dump compost. I'm screaming for help. All I was trying to do was aid this woman and now she has betrayed me. Fear is now anger. I claw desperately at the loose soil, ready to claw out her eyes if I make it out of here alive. My feet are covered with dirt and garbage as she continues to bury me with whatever is around these dumping pits. As if it couldn't get worse, it begins to rain. It's one of those vicious Texas thunderstorms that rolls in so fast you don't know it was even there before it's directly above your head.

I want my husband. I want my life before this wicked thing stumbled into my reality. The harder it rains the muddier the hole gets. My body is sinking deeper into the earth, ready for it to swallow me whole. The pit is filling fast. I scramble harder, trying to dig, but the more I fight the faster I sink. The fetid watery stew is up to my neck. She is still watching me, howling, screeching. Can anyone hear her, or me? Not over this rain and thunder. I'm sure I will die alone with this creature watching every last second. My feet are fastened to the ground when the water overtakes my lungs.

★　　★　　★

"Can you hear me? Please say something. I'm so sorry it had to be this way."

I am now standing over the pit, looking down at my long hair splayed in the water with my arms floating above. My body looks like a jellyfish in a trash-filled ocean.

Diana, the Donkey Lady, is next to me. But I can hear her speak. We communicate through the language of death. I look at her bitterly. My instinct is to kick her as hard as I can. "Why did you murder me? I tried to help you!"

"I know. I am horrible, but I do need your help. And I'm lonely. Everyone sees me as a joke, a stupid urban legend."

The look on her bruised and beaten face strips me of my anger. There is only pity because I know this face was not of her own making. Someone did this to her. My tone softens. "You've taken my life. What more could you possibly want?"

She looks deeper into the woods, then to her keloid-striped hands. Tears streak her dusty face. "I want revenge on those who did this to me. You saw the video. It was more excruciating than you could ever imagine. The video didn't show half of the things they did to me."

"Why couldn't I help you alive? There are police, my husband. I could have done more for you alive than dead."

"No, I'm afraid you couldn't. There are those who are alive who need to be punished, but they're being protected by the dead. I needed a dead companion, a true friend. You were a friend to me. I'm sorry. I'll never forgive myself, and I know at some point I'll answer for what I've done, but when you're desperate and there seems to be no other way, you would do anything."

I remember that desperation. My own mother had the same desperation when she picked up my sister and me after school. We wondered why all our belongings made us sit in the backseat of our car with our tiny legs squashed to the point we couldn't move. When we were sound asleep, she was driving so fast she hit a patch of black ice in Oklahoma, overturning our Jeep Cherokee. We were all okay, though, her desperation could have gotten us all killed. I don't think she ever forgave herself for that. I would help Diana as this ghost I now was.

"If we're going to do this, I need to know your story."

She howls and wipes her wet nose and eyes the best she can with her mangled hands. "Some of the story is correct. I was a curandera and my husband a curandero. We had a business that was very successful until he decided he wanted more. More power, more control, more of everything. He sacrificed me to get it."

I turn away from my dead body and look into the forest. "What are we up against, then?"

She howls again and rests her head against my waist. "The spirit of a dead curandero that has been promised a body for casting spells between worlds. He's channeling the will of evil men, serial killers, to continue to make stronger black magic."

"What can I do? I don't know anything about magic or defeating evil."

"I'll teach you. For now, we will find them, and you'll see for yourself."

★ ★ ★

We return to the bridge. I now know why this is where she resides. This isn't just some bridge in a small town with a fun legend to tell in the dark. It's a bridge between worlds. The creek beneath is a black sludge that looks like a sheet of latex flowing the opposite direction the water should run. Faces and limbs poke through, stretching, wailing. Occasional bubbles form, then float into the atmosphere, then burst, releasing a plume of white dust that dissipates as it leaves my sight.

"What the fuck is this place?" I say in disbelief.

"It's the bridge." She whispers so as not to disturb the spirits or call attention to us.

"In Texas?"

"Yes. Since prehistoric times there have been humans here.

It's said a healer established a village here for people with a special connection to the spirit world. He, or they, opened a space between worlds. As life was very hard back then, they didn't survive or were scattered, some probably absorbed into other tribes. The portal never closed. Things come and go from the river all the time. That's why there are so many legends in Texas."

All those things my abuela told me were true.

We watch another bubble burst in the air. A distorted toothless face whips a forked tongue at us then disappears. She cowers behind me. "Together we'll find the spirit of the shaman so he may help us. But first we'll travel so you may see my enemies."

I listen to her speak as I watch cars come and go, not seeing us or knowing we are there. I had been one of those people, but no longer. I wonder, when they find my body, what they will call me. What story will be told about my death on this bridge? Yesterday I was Jackie; today I am the Lady in the Pit.

NIGHTMARES & ICE

The child would not stop wailing. No amount of bouncing, breastfeeding, singing, or blasting the radio would stop the infant from screaming. Ariela's head ached from the baby crying for hours in the car that she couldn't leave because they were homeless. The security guard in the twenty-four-hour Walmart followed her because she walked around in loops without so much as a single item in her cart. She left before he threw her out or called the cops. Cops meant ICE.

Five dollars. Only five dollars to choose gas or food. Wishing she had a choice in all this made her feel desperate and angry. The desperation felt like claws so deeply attached to her skull, any sudden movements would scalp her without warning. There would be no sudden movements because there were no choices before and even fewer now that she had this little human who depended on her completely. All she wanted to do was get her child to sleep so she could close her eyes for a few hours before looking for work again in the morning. It would have to be something she could do without childcare and still breastfeed. If there was no work, she would attempt to secure a place in a shelter again. They were always so full by the time the day labor jobs were filled.

Things had to change. She looked at the yellow lamp above her car blotted by insects. She gritted her teeth, tasting tears and snot on her lips.

"I need a change. I need something. Anything. Please!" she screamed at the parking lot light as if it were a telephone line to God.

After another twenty minutes the infant finally stopped crying. Ariela's eyes began to shut when a loud thud came from the roof of her car. She looked at both doors to make sure they were locked. There was just enough gas to park somewhere else if it was someone looking for trouble.

When she turned her face towards the windshield, there it was. The body was the size of a large dog covered in black feathers. Thin, branch-like legs were rings of hard flesh capped by talons the size of the head of a baby. The sharp points were caked in mud and what appeared to be strings of flesh. But that wasn't the worst part. The face on the body was that of a human.

It could only mean one thing: that the story was not a story after all. How many times had she been told that tale to make her behave? La Lechuza, the nightmare told to scare children at night, the thing that tears families apart by carrying crying children away never to be seen again. Ariela remembered that story so well.

The parking lot light was bright enough that every horrid feature could be seen. Its eyes were red with yellow rings surrounding the vertical black slits for pupils. There was a gaping hole of rotten flesh where the nose should be. But it was the mouth that made Ariela feel like she was in the presence of evil. Tinted the same shade as crushed dried chilis, cracked lips spread almost ear to ear across its face. The corners of the mouth each had a triangular membrane that would allow it to extend the length of its jaw with teeth as mangled as shattered glass starting beneath the lips and extending as far back into its throat as Ariela could see. It was a vortex of pain leading to a place where screams don't escape. Tufts of matted hair of different lengths sprouted from its scalp. Ariela started her car without strapping the baby in the car seat.

"My dear, don't be frightened, I'm here to help. You look thin and hungry."

Ariela was not expecting it to talk and speak with such a calm abuelita-like voice. She revved the engine in defiance, hoping to scare it off. "What do you want, bruja?"

"I want to help you. Yes, I'm a witch, but I'm a witch that can bring you fortune. Come with me."

Ariela squeezed her baby tighter. "I know the story. You eat babies. No way I'm coming with you. Fuck off!"

The creature began to retch. Its body shook violently until it vomited two gold coins onto the hood of the car. "There's much more where that came from. You see, I'm very old and have no use for things like riches even though I have come across so many of them in my time. I am just a lonely old woman in need of assistance every now and again. Come with me to my humble home and you can have whatever you wish."

Ariela could not stop looking at the gold on her car. It glowed underneath the light. It could be the miracle she needed. A squawk from the creature broke the hypnotic lure of the treasure. What was she even thinking, contemplating this deal with a witch, or devil? But she was exhausted, hungry, and her milk supply was low because she didn't have enough food for herself, and there was no way she could afford formula. Her last five dollars. The only other things she had of value were this car, the bowie knife with a turquoise and mother of pearl handle, and her body. The last thought made her shudder.

She breathed in her baby's scent. "For you, mija, my world. You will have as many choices as you could possibly want."

Her mother had told her the same thing when they crossed the border when she was five years old. Ariela barely missed getting picked up by ICE a month ago. Her parents were not so lucky. She didn't know where they were. Did her mother have her heart medication? Would those bastards at least have some humanity, a heart?

"Where do you live, bruja?"

La Lechuza let out a cackle, showing her teeth again. "Just at the edge of the park. Past the last set of missions."

The missions near Espada Park had been there since Texas was still part of Mexico. There were so many weird tales of the things that lurked around there at night. That was why Ariela felt safe there. No one would be looking for them in a place like that, the edge of where one world clashed with another so long ago.

She strapped her daughter into the secondhand baby carrier and placed a pacifier in her mouth. As a precaution, she tucked the leather-sheathed knife in her jeans behind her back.

"Mama, Papa, La Virgen, Jesus, please help me. Please let this be the answer to my prayers. I need a miracle." Ariela turned off the engine and cautiously stepped out of the car.

La Lechuza took to the air. "Here, lovely, take these coins as a gesture of good faith."

The coins were coated with a thick mucus, but they looked and felt real. The gold was pliable. Whatever was once imprinted on them had almost worn off. They were old.

The creature took flight, guiding Ariela with the baby carrier in hand. They walked over a small hill into a ditch that led to an open cement drain big enough to walk through if you crouched slightly. The smell made Ariela's empty stomach turn and grind with acid.

"I'm sorry for the stench; it's my own doing. I feed on small rodents, that's all. I was hoping you could help me clear it out. I can remove the carcasses, but I can't clean all that's left over. 'Tis easy to manage some things with my mouth, but not everything. Over the centuries I often need humans to help me with duties I cannot perform. It's part of my curse." A broom stood next to the opening.

Ariela grabbed the broom and followed la Lechuza. As they ventured deeper into the drain, Ariela could sense something was wrong. The baby began to fuss, and mice ran past her towards the entrance. The stench of rot and feces was dizzying. They reached a point where four drains met and a gated hole above their heads allowed more light into the drainage system. Ariela dropped the broom. The space was littered with carcasses of all sizes oozing fluids and filth.

"What's wrong, lovely? Are you scared? You're all the same: lured by shiny things to a place you don't belong." The creature extended its wings and showed the full size of its mouth, which was large enough to devour a small child of at least six years old.

Ariela dropped the baby carrier, causing the infant to scream. The wailing was a deafening echo. How stupid she felt thinking her luck could change, that this world would give anything to anyone like her. How could she think she deserved good things? Her father made his way in this country on his own, asking nothing from anyone, and what did he get in return? She thought of all those choices denied her.

Now she had a choice. This thing, this eater of the poor, the desperate, the down-and-out; Ariela would kill this thing. With every ounce of hate from watching the ICE officers throw her father to the pavement and twist her mother's arm roughly with tears in her eyes, she grabbed the knife from her back and charged towards the creature.

With all her body weight, she knocked the creature down and straddled la Lechuza. It screeched in terror and pain. Ariela drove her father's hunting knife through its soft body. As the baby screamed its helpless cry, Ariela released all her rage, regret, disappointment, self-loathing and sorrow. All her emotions stabbed directly into the heart of la Lechuza. Her violent screams drowned those of her daughter. When the tip of the knife broke from repeatedly hitting concrete, she began to rip the thing with her bare hands, pulling out whatever organ was caught in her grasp. Blood, feathers and viscera flew into the air, covering the young woman. Her arms ached from the vicious attack until only a feathered, bloody carcass remained.

The sun was rising, filling the sewer with light. Ariela could see piles of discarded items from la Lechuza's victims. There was also a pile of bones of all sizes in another corner. Ariela felt no remorse for killing this thing that had been a plague, feeding on desperation. She gave her baby a bloody kiss and shushed her quietly. Her daughter smiled and cooed in return.

As Ariela began to leave, a frigid gust brushed against her back. Ariela shivered, tightening her grip on her daughter.

A soft voice called out, "This way."

She had seen all the films before; there was no way she was going to listen. She continued to leave, but something pulled on her shirt. Ariela looked at her feet. From the corner of her eye, and moved by a force not seen, a chest the size of a backpack slid towards her heels. The chest looked old, nearly rotting away in parts. But something glinted in the stream of light.

Ariela kneeled in the bloody, dirty water, forgetting her fear momentarily. What was once a lock was now a rusted mass of metal. She carefully opened the rotten chest. What was in it was pure gold. It was full of dust and some of it was caked with dirt and God knows what else, but it was real. There were nuggets, flattened pieces that looked like jewelry from civilizations long gone, and smooth discs that must have been coins at one time. There were also newer pieces of jewelry, watches.

"Take it. Thank you for freeing us." Another gust of wind caught her hair as it made its way through the opening of the drains.

She looked around but saw nothing there except a mouse scurrying in the dark. The infant was no longer crying. She grabbed the carrier handle with her free arm and walked out of that tomb. She couldn't pay for gas with gold that looked like it was taken from a museum or with a sack of watches. She didn't know what to do with it. One look at her and they would probably arrest her on the spot. She had lived here since she was a small child, however she was still illegal in the eyes of the law. Not a day in her life did her family need public assistance. The only reason her father, a carpenter, was taken was because a client tried to undercut him on a job already completed. When her father refused the payment below the agreed-upon amount, an anonymous tip was reported to the authorities about a bunch of illegals.

She would have to find someone who would give her cash immediately and had enough of it. There would be no authorities because they would just take her treasure, her baby and any future she might have. The neighborhood dealer was the first person who came to mind. She only knew who this man was because her father always warned her to stay away. But if she could handle a centuries-old creature, what was some guy selling weed?

Before the morning beckoned people to the park, Ariela changed her clothes and cleaned herself with baby wipes in the public toilet.

Ariela waited until noon before going to the dealer's house to give the inhabitants time to wake up. She sat parked on the opposite side of the street until she could hear music playing and saw the door open to allow a little chihuahua with three legs outside. She fed the baby to keep her calm, then approached the house.

A man with a spiderweb tattooed on one side of his neck and praying hands on the other opened the door. He wore a white guayabera with Dickies. Just like her dad, white socks with grandpa slippers.

"What can I do for a nice girl like you?"

"I'm not fucking nice. I'm here on business. I found some stuff and I need as much money as I can get."

He looked her up and down. "I've seen you before. Walking the baby around. Doesn't your dad have his own business? Yeah, I heard about ICE getting at your parents. The whole neighborhood watched that. They trying to put the fear of the president in us. Come in."

The house smelled of weed and empanada dough.

"What can I help you with today?"

Ariela showed him the chest and backpack filled with other items. He rifled through the contents, scrunching his face as his hands became coated with dirt and dried blood. "The fuck is this?"

"Don't ask. But I need to unload all of it for cash. As soon as possible."

He looked at the baby and back at Ariela. He clearly had a ton of questions but knew that was not what she needed right then. "Okay. Some of this I can hit my cousin up for. He works at a pawn shop on the south side. The other, older stuff...you heard of the Dark Web? You can sell stuff on it, like eBay, but bad shit or shit you don't want traced. My homie Ricky will hook you up. Where are you staying?"

Ariela wanted to look tough, but this question made her shrink to the size of a penny. She had been in her car parked across the street after returning from the grocery store when ICE dragged her parents out of their home. The officers were screaming about other people living there. Her father looked right at her when he shouted that there was no one else. Just them. The officers didn't believe him and warned they would be watching the place. She returned in the middle of the night to retrieve as much as she could fit into her car. None of her parents' bank cards worked as their assets had been frozen. It wasn't long until she drained her own account. After two weeks the locks were changed on the house with an eviction notice on the doors. "I don't have a place. I'm scared to go home because of ICE."

He pulled out a wad of cash. "Fuck those motherfuckers. Get yourself a room at the La Quinta and Ricky will be over tomorrow to get you started. I'll tell him to get you the number of a center that can help with your parents. Take care, mujer."

*   *   *

Ariela had tears in her eyes, watching her daughter run into the classroom in her uniform. She took photos for her parents, who were at home. It took about a month, and a lot of cash, but she managed to get her parents out of ICE custody. Seeing them for the first time made her heart turn ice cold. They weren't in good health. But thank God for nightmares in the night, because it ended well for them. Today was the first day of school for her daughter and the rest of her little life. Not only did Ariela pay a full year of tuition upfront, she would be able to keep her daughter in private school for the foreseeable future. She wanted to continue to watch her giggle in excitement, but she had to run before her own classes began. It was a class she was enjoying too, Anthropology and Mythical Creatures of Mexico. Ariela couldn't wait to begin her research on a book she had decided to write.

CAM GIRL SALLY

I worked from ten p.m. to three a.m. unless a regular wanted a specific time. That was always extra. After Mom left me for the night, without all her fussing and hand-wringing worry, I could breathe again. That was my time to make some real dinero that would get me out of my pit of hospital bills and student loan debt. Mom said she would take extra shifts to save for another surgery, but what she made in a week I could make in a weekend.

All that's behind me now as I sit in this sterile room in a hospital gown.

When I return home, my masks will still be hanging on the wall in my bedroom. They're my many faces for my many lovers, even though I'm still a virgin – not by choice. I guess I should have slept with what's-his-face on prom night.

Despite never experiencing physical love with another person, I sure as hell know how to experience it with myself. That's what they paid me the big dollars for. I used to be a cam girl. I was the girl in the mask and costume of your choosing. Tell me your fantasy, I always listened. You could watch me dance around my bedroom before I lay on my bed to show you all the ways I like to be pleasured. Judge me, hate me, call me what you will, but it was the only thing that kept us afloat after 'the incident'.

Three years ago, I was in college, had a part-time job at the school library, and was seeing the cute guy in my bio class. After our third date, I decided he would be my first. Then some motherfucker, not even a student, gets it into his loco-ass mind to shoot up my campus. I can't even remember the reason for it and his name doesn't matter. I'll spit on his grave even when I'm long dead. Anyway, as soon as I heard the first rapid shots, I knew what was happening. We all did. We all wore the same terror on our faces as we looked at each other for reassurance or help. I dropped my bag, my phone, and ran. I ran until my kneecaps felt like they would pop off my legs and I'd vomit my lungs. But the fear kept me going, the fear of being a photograph next to a candle at some vigil on TV. Maybe I should have done track in high school, because I wasn't fast enough to outrun one of his bullets.

Everyone, every damn person, tells me how lucky I am to be alive. The bullet missed my brain and major arteries only to shatter the left side of my face. I woke up feeling like the dentist in *Little Shop of Horrors* had a good go on my jaw. I could only see out of one eye because the other had to be removed. The first time I looked in a mirror I thought I looked like a Q-tip. Surely it couldn't be that bad underneath. My life was normal one minute and the next like scattered gray matter and skull fragments on cement at a crime scene.

The media wanted interviews, someone set up a GoFundMe page to help the survivors. We had food, flowers and cash dropped off for weeks, but it doesn't take long for people to move on and forget. People's charity only goes so far. And fuck 'thoughts and prayers'; they don't do shit. The money runs out, my student loan grace period ends, rent needs to be paid, medication needs to be purchased, hospitals want their money for my extended stay. So yeah, I'm lucky. I'm lucky to be saddled with nonstop pain in my jaw, a face I don't recognize, and so much debt there were days I only ate one meal. It would break my mom's heart if I ever told her that.

That's when I decided to get a bit entrepreneurial. My best friend, Patricia, and her boyfriend, Frank, came over the day I finally didn't need pain medication anymore. Since the bandages came off, I'd resorted to wearing a thin, black balaclava that was supposed to help with the scarring. It didn't prevent me from drooling everywhere when my facial muscles decided to spasm from nerve damage. I wore a patch to cover my missing eye. No longer a Q-Tip, but rather a bank-robbing pirate.

We drank ourselves blind, or at least until we started talking nonsense. I asked them what the hell I was going to do now.

Patricia joked that I should strip and quipped, "Have you seen them bitches at the Scratching Post?"

Frank, not just drunk, but also high, says, "Nah, be a cam girl. I'll do your website for free. Wear a freaking mask. I dunno. There's something for everyone out there."

We all laughed and passed out. The next day I couldn't get the idea out of my head. I wanted to do it. It took Frank two days to set me up with used equipment and a website. Patricia and I bought a bunch of cheap outfits and masks on eBay over a bottle of wine. Money was tight that month with that initial investment. You gotta spend money to make money, right?

Lucky for me, my body was left perfect. I didn't have so much as a scraped knee when they loaded me into the ambulance. I'm on the shorter side, but I've got those voluptuous mestiza curves that give the most pious of men whiplash. My skin is the color of oak-aged rum. Before each show, I slather myself with bronzer and cocoa butter until it glows. It's only my face that's a horror. My cam name was Sally because, like Sally from *The Nightmare Before Christmas*, my face is a stitched-up patchwork, hence the masks. But Sally is so much more beautiful than me. I feel like Leatherface. Until today, the hate and self-pity inside was a slow decaying monstrosity.

At first, I was shy, not really sure if anyone would visit my page. Boy, was I wrong. Never doubt how many freaks are in the world with even freakier predilections. The more requests I received, the more I could put myself in the mood for a show good enough to keep them coming back. My playlist for the evening depended on my mood. Once the music began, I'd forget I even had a mask on or there was a camera connected to someone I've never met. Fingertips traced all the places I wanted touched, but with no one around to do it for me. It felt good to be seen and invisible at the same time. It also felt good to just get off. I fantasized about my Instagram crushes, sex in exotic places, anything to give me that release. I'm my only comfort as long as I look like this. I'll never forget all the people that whispered, "She was such a beautiful girl. What a shame." To my customers, I was still beautiful.

But it wasn't all bad. My regulars were pretty cool, if paying to watch a young woman masturbate in a panda mask, cheap French maid uniform and torn fishnets is cool. They'd ask me how my day was going, and if it was a bad day, I'd tell them. Perhaps that impersonal transaction made us both feel less lonely. I got a P.O. box where some of them sent me cards, stuffed animals, clothes, chocolates. If they knew I needed a bit of extra cash they'd offer to buy my masks after I'd worn them. I really don't want to know what they did with them…. Hey, every dime helped though, because I wasn't going to do that forever. The plan was to save enough for a top plastic surgeon to look at my face. I was desperate. Desperate for love, for hope, to return to school to become a counselor, for anything to get me out of that shithole apartment with my mom. I wanted to live again. I didn't survive 'that day'; I died and just went to a place between life and death. But everybody's luck changes. God can't ignore all prayers.

Then it happened. Right before I logged off, a little beep notified me I had a new message.

Hey, love the photos. Your body is smoking hot. How old are you?

I had one more dance in me, so I responded, *Old enough. I promise.*

Okay, give me a show. I want the Halloween witch mask and some black lace lingerie.

That little fifteen minutes meant rent would be paid on time.

Make your payment and let's get started.

The routine was lazy and I opted to fake it. The guy gave me the impression he didn't care if I or any woman orgasmed. We signed off after I finished and that was going to be the end of that.

The following evening it was the same guy at the same time.

Remove your mask. I need to see the face that goes with that body.

I told him no, yet he continued to push for more. *Can I hear your voice? How can we make this more intimate? Do you mind if I wear a mask? I find it exciting.*

Okay, but it's extra, I typed.

I flipped on the function on my computer so we could hear each other and now I could see him. We were both wearing masks. He wore a navy terry cloth robe and a child's wolf mask, the kind that covers only your face and is held in place by a thin white elastic band. How dull. Because my face was covered, he would never know how boring it was to hear him drone on about himself coupled with unoriginal dirty talk. His voice seemed a little familiar though; then again, it was late.

In my boredom, I looked around at what appeared to be his home office. It was decorated in an old-fashioned, old-money kind of way in heavy, ornately carved wood, lots of books – probably only there for show, and shiny picture frames. One of the pictures caught my eye as the men in it seemed familiar. I took a screenshot of the man in the mask and the room. We finished our conversation and he selected another mask and outfit for me to perform in. Before we signed off, he told me he wanted to send me something special in the mail.

The masked client's package arrived after three days. I opened a purple box that smelled of jasmine and rose. Delicate black tissue paper and a silky ribbon tied in a bow covered the gift inside. Expensive shit. It was a purple La Perla chemise. The mask was a black leather thing that covered my entire head with only pinpricks to see through. There was a matching detachable purple ball gag attached to the mouth hole. Hey, whatever floats your boat, as long as you keep mine above water.

He wanted to talk again before my show. He was in the same room, but at a different angle. I got a full view of the picture that caught my eye before. It was the president shaking the hand of the senator of my state. Why would anyone have a picture of that in their house?

It started as a small thought, but it clicked. I remember thinking: If *this* guy is the senator from my state, this shitbag is going down. I'm going to stick him until he bleeds green. This guy was one of the reasons I look the way I do. His voting record was the reason my shooter was armed that day. I couldn't touch the shooter, but I could do something about the guy who held his cock in front of me, spilling all his filthy garbage to a woman in a mask while he sips on high-end alcohol without a care in the world. I buttered him up enough to keep him talking about himself, making sure I recorded everything and taking as many detailed screenshots as possible.

The next day I played YouTube videos of his speeches followed by the recording I had of my masked client. They had to be the same person. I let Patricia listen. She was just as convinced that it was Senator Gordon. For the first time in a long time, I felt like I had some control. I had come up with a plan. I was going to convince him to take off his mask.

I spent weeks grooming him. Sweet talk, ego stroking, dirty talk, using every single sex toy I owned, plus a few new ones to keep his interest. After three weeks I felt confident enough to take the shot.

"I bet you are so hot underneath that mask. Can't I get one little look? You're practically my boyfriend now!" I purred.

"No can do, sexy. I could get into big trouble. I don't want to sound like an ass, but I'm pretty important. Those nice things I send you aren't cheap."

I clenched my jaw and gritted my teeth with his bullshit. I wanted to slap the mask right off his face and shove it down his throat. Instead, I giggled.

"You don't trust me? I promise to make it worth your while. I'll do anything you want."

He hung his head and moaned. My legs shook rapidly underneath my desk while sweat made my silk kimono cling to my skin. *Take it off!* I shrieked inside my head.

He raised his head back towards the camera. "Okay. I'll take it off if you meet me in person. I want to play for real. I need to see if you're really a virgin."

Fuck, fuck, dammit, cocksucker, jerk! But I didn't scream those words. I composed myself. Thank God for my masks, so he wouldn't see me on the verge of tears. This was going to work. I knew I could count on Patricia to help. Together we're chingona as hell, and this pig was going to squeal money all over me. For a moment I wondered if it might not be the senator. Maybe he's some rich guy that has this photo in his home office for an unknown reason. No, I had to take that risk.

"Okay. My apartment this weekend. You can have me for free. I like you that much. Maybe I'm even falling for you." I laid it on real thick, like a handful of petroleum jelly. *Doubt me if you dare, pendejo. Mama is coming for you*, I thought, smiling inside like I did before the shooting.

Didn't these guys ever learn? Didn't they know dirty fingers always leave stains? This was my opportunity to drain this bastard for everything I needed to clear my debt and pay for surgery. I'd recorded and kept everything that had happened between us over those last three weeks. My mom was working overtime again so I knew the apartment would be free.

Patricia hid in my closet to record our exchange. When I gave the code phrase, "Come give it to me, Daddy," she would jump out and let the prick know she was recording. Frank hid in the kitchen in case we needed backup. I prayed it would go smoothly.

It was the day of my big plan. I almost didn't want to answer the door. My bladder ached even though I didn't need to pee and my heart beat like I had just downed three shots of espresso. I made sure to wear another one of his fancy lingerie sets, get my nails done, hair freshly styled by Patricia: it was a half updo that concealed a small knife in case he had trouble getting the message. I looked hot for a woman in a witch's mask.

Then I heard the knock. *Forgive me, Father, for I know exactly what I am doing.* I answered the door to a man wearing a wolf mask.

"Come in." I grabbed him by the hand to hurry things along; there was no reason to prolong the pain. I'm really a nice person after all.

He looked around before entering the apartment. Once the door shut behind him, he removed his mask. It was the senator. I was right. I was fucking right! I'd never wanted sex more than that moment, just not with him. He eyed me like a kid staring at a sack of candy on Halloween night.

"Okay. I've held up my end of the deal. Your turn." He flashed a smile with perfectly aligned and polished teeth that looked fake. Green eyes like an algae-covered pond poured over my body. He tried to grab my breasts, but I walked backward until I crossed the threshold of my room. Patricia would have a clear shot. He was trying to take off his clothes while already deflowering me with his eyes. I needed to get information while he was unmasked to verify everything else I had on him.

"Why don't I give you a real show first? A bit of foreplay, just like we've been doing for weeks now. How many times have you paid for it? Now you can have it for free. I'm all yours."

He stepped closer, placing a hand on my waist. "Oh, baby, I can't wait. The last few weeks have made me so crazy. I can't seem to concentrate on anything. But if you promise to give me something special, maybe I'll wait a little longer."

I smiled as much as I could with my scars. "Okay. Come give it to me, Daddy."

Patricia leapt out of my closet so he could see the camera filming. She also had a baseball bat in the other hand in case he wanted to run.

I took off my mask so he could see my face. My left eye is a hollow black socket of puckered raw skin. Thick scars run from the left side of my mouth along my jaw, all the way to my ear. My left cheek is like a shriveled apple with a large bite taken from the middle. The left side of my nose is reduced to melted candle wax. There's a scar parallel to my hairline that's so pronounced it looks like you could peel off my face like a fruit roll-up.

He screamed and stumbled against the wall.

"Not so fast, my Sancho. We still need to play." I unleashed my hair by pulling out the knife.

He tried to scramble towards the door. "Don't come near me! Your face. Whatever you want you can have, just let me go."

I followed him. "Anything? Okay. I want the best doctors. I want my student loans paid. I want my fucking life back!" He was lucky Patricia held the bat, because I might have bashed his brain in at that moment. It took all my strength not to gut him with my blade. All the tears I cried as I called out in ecstasy while alone, all the anger I felt in my agonizing pain as I recovered, made me temporarily forget law and order even existed.

"You're going to transfer me everything I need, or I'll go on the record with all our conversations, videos of you pleasuring yourself for me, all of it. And of course, today was recorded, thanks to my homegirl here."

Patricia approached us and placed a folded piece of paper with the amount I wanted in his hand.

"How do I know you won't keep asking for more?"

I got right in his face so he could see the great big hole in my head. His eyes reflected the terror I saw the day of the shooting when the first shots rang out. I pressed my breasts against his chest so he could feel my hardened nipples and understand how excited I was to see him helpless. I was the one holding the weapon. The mixture of anger and power made the thin lace between my thighs sticky.

Close to his ear I whispered, "I'm not greedy. I just want what I need to get my life back."

The bastard couldn't even look at me. His sweat stank, so I moved away from him. I took the blade to the thin straps of the chemise he sent me to remove it from my body. It fit nicely down his unzipped jeans. Never in my life had I ever felt so confident, even with my scarred face. I was a nude Aztec priestess standing over my sacrificial captive.

His demeanor was that of a defeated man. "Fine."

I let him leave with Frank escorting him out. Patricia, my ride-or-die homegirl, and I drank until we passed out on my floor.

The next day I checked my bank balance. Everything was there. I turned my music loud enough to disturb the neighbors so I could dance around my room with no one watching. Then I remembered, it was time for the news. I only promised the good senator I wouldn't ask him for more money. Not once did I say I wouldn't pass on my evidence to the local news station anonymously. Who would have guessed? Dreams do come true in America.

DANCEHALL DEVIL

They say she is a beauty, with hair that will tangle you in tendrils of brown as you spin her around. Before you know it, you are as helpless as a spider's next meal. Her lips are so wet and inviting you might mistake them for forbidden fruit you can't help but want to taste. That shine is poison. Eyes are obsidian. Black as a sky without a moon or stars. You will be forever lost and forget you ever wanted anything else but her if you stare too long. But it is her feet that are the tell-tale sign you are dancing with the devil. She will bury your bones beneath hooves of a goat stained with blood that looks like nail polish. This is just what they say. I tend bar at the dancehall where she was last seen, and let me tell you, she is very real.

This is what happened when that devil of a woman walked in with her friends.

It was Friday night, payday. It was crowded with men and women wanting to unwind from a hard week or hope to find an easy fuck. Both are good enough reasons to come out. The band plays merengue and salsa every Friday. It's a crowd of Wrangler jeans, hats, tight dresses and boots. The music is loud and hot, something they would play in hell because the bodies are packed so tight there is no room between them. Grinding bodies, slithering bodies, bodies that should be in a motel room because their mouths are kissing so passionately you wonder why they aren't already naked. As the night wears on, the more drinks stream down gullets, the more freedom everyone feels.

Every bar has its regulars. Most of them are nice, respectful, leave a little tip for the lady working weekends so she can save for college for her teenage son. Then there was that one. That one who felt entitled to every woman who passed by. The one who always wanted to pick a fight if a dude looked at him wrong. He was a bully of the worst kind. No matter how many times I complained to management about the comments he made to me or other patrons, I was told as long as he was a paying customer, his money was good enough here. None of the bar staff, male or female, wanted to serve him. It goes without saying, he always came in alone.

A group of five women stood at the bar. Each wore a dress in a different color with a matching faux flower in their hair half pinned up. Their makeup and hairstyle were both old-school, like they'd walked out of the 1940s; classic pachucas, so beautiful and timeless. They toasted with shots of Mezcal while dancing in place and chatting with each other.

Paulo walked past me. "I'm going on break. You know who just walked in. I want to keep my job, so you deal with him. Last time I almost jumped over the bar and punched him in the face."

I rolled my eyes. Paulo was good people. He didn't need trouble so I wouldn't hold this sudden abandonment against him. This job was paying for his wife's notary classes.

The troublesome customer decided to shoulder his way to the bar next to the group of five women. He looked them up and down, not even trying to disguise his lust.

"Oye, baby. Let me buy you a drink." He chose to bother the woman in red. Her dress was off the shoulders with a ruffle over the bust, fitted to the waist then fell loose just above the knee.

She stared at him hard so he would get the message. "No thank you, vato. I'm here with friends."

I could feel something about to happen. It was nearly midnight and he was already decently drunk.

He slipped his hand to the side of her hip.

She turned her head to the side again, eyes narrowing. They looked completely black to me, but I thought it was a trick of the light. Her friends stopped their conversation and drinking. "I said no, cabron. I'm here with my friends and I want to have a good time."

He positioned his body so that he was standing directly behind her, too close for a total stranger. "Baby, I'll show you a good time. Once I'm inside of you. I got my truck outside with an extended cab. Just a dance first. I know you chicks like foreplay."

I expected her to walk away or call security. How could any woman allow a man to talk to her like that? But was I any better for not speaking up? What could I do? All my complaints went ignored.

She looked at her silent friends, who watched expressionless, their eyes dead as the beer sign behind me reflected in the sheen of the blackness of their eyes. In unison they nodded to their friend in red.

"Okay, hombre, you think you know what I want? Come dance with me. Then maybe I will let you inside as you so romantically put it."

The man made my stomach turn. His cologne smelled worse than his machismo. I wanted to stab him with a corkscrew or string him up with his bolo tie. A smug smile stretched across his face. You could tell he thought he had won.

He wrenched the woman's arm to the dance floor and forcefully pulled her hips to his own. Their bodies twisted and turned as he grinded against her, trying to show off, but it was when he tried to squeeze her ass that things got interesting.

As his fingers worked to pull up her dress, she grabbed his hand with such force the bones in his fingers crumbled. It looked like she held a rubber glove. She began to lead the dance over his screams while the band played a merengue song. They spun faster and faster, so fast they looked like an out-of-control top made of hair and red fabric. People cleared the way so as not to get knocked over. She just laughed over his cries for help. The band quit their playing as they watched.

Then a scream.

Her dress floated like a bright hibiscus flower in full bloom, showing her thong and thighs, but that wasn't what made the band stop playing or caused the people to scream. The bottom half of her legs were those of a goat. Her feet were cloven hooves with a spiked horn jutting from the back of each. When she noticed the band had stopped, she and her four friends looked their way.

The singer panicked and shouted into the microphone, "¡Uno, dos, tres!"

A horn started a new song. The four women joined her on the dance floor. Their legs and feet were those of a goat, too. They danced around the man, laughing, shouting gritos, with their thongs, thighs and fishnet stockings held up by garters in full view, not caring who saw because they were having the time of their lives.

How I wanted to join them. To spin in merengue oblivion. It must be just as satisfying to dance around your tormentor in pain as it is to dance on their grave.

As he begged for them to stop, his dance partner unfurled a forked tongue as long as a whip. His eyes widened upon seeing it float in front of his face. He didn't know what it would do next. With the quickness of a scorpion's pinch, it plucked out his eyes. Blood oozed from the empty sockets as he screamed for help, but there was no one to come to his aid. The other women had tongues just as long and teased the man by whipping his body or lapping up his blood. When he could no longer stand, they stopped their dance. The band threw down their instruments and ran out the door.

The five women stood in a circle, looking down on the crushed man. The woman in red put one cloven hoof on his belly. "I won't kill you but now you may never have the pleasure or privilege of looking at or touching another woman again."

There were sounds of sirens approaching. I waved my hands in the air to get the goat women's attention. They turned their heads towards me then galloped on their hooves to the back of the bar.

"This way. Come quick!" Before leaving, the woman in red pulled out a one-hundred-dollar bill from beneath the bust of her dress. "Until next time." She gave me a wink that almost made me fall in love with her.

Now, Friday night is Ladies' Night and men are always on their best behavior.

STREET FIGHTER

We all have our secrets. Some we keep to ourselves and take to the grave; others we share with another. You don't speak of it or try to think of it, but it's always there in the back of your mind to remind you of the time you did that thing.

I was fifteen years old when I took possession of my first secret. My mother and I were driving home from my grandmother's house. We tried to visit her as often as possible to bring her groceries or fried fish from her favorite fast food joint if we could afford it. If I remember correctly, it was about dusk. My baby sister was at home with the sitter who lived next door, Mercedes.

As we approached our shared home, we could see a commotion in the street. It was a pile of men fighting like rabid animals trying to get the biggest bite of a fresh kill. Their clothes were torn, and some had blood on their faces. Brown bodies tumbled with hash marks scratched in their skin and clothing. People with blank faces watched the spectacle from their yards as dogs barked and snarled behind fences or tied to trees. No one did anything to intervene.

But this was no ordinary street fight. The closer we were, the clearer the scene. There was a man in the center of the fray. His nose looked broken with blood running from both nostrils into his mouth. One eye had no white left, only red. He was getting the shit kicked out of him in the middle of a road that was usually quiet. I don't know why but my mother stopped our car.

"Get in!" she shouted through her open window.

The man receiving the blows from the crowd broke free,

ripping the last of his shirt from the grasp of a guy with his belt wrapped around his knuckles. He jumped into the backseat. My mother pressed hard on the gas to speed away. I turned back to look at the crowd. A priest was running towards our car screaming, "No!" with his arms waving wildly above his head. He dropped to his knees as we left them all behind.

I turned my attention to the man, who was adjusting his out-of-place nose. The sound made me shiver. When he lifted his head from the floor and looked into my eyes, I knew we were in trouble.

You see it in movies; the killer has this maniacal look on his face, or his eyes are devoid of life. There was nothing in this man's eyes. All I could see was my own reflection. The sanguine in one eye moved around like a lava lamp, making him appear like an alien or demon. He rested both his hands on his knees as he stared back at me. Blood continued to drip from both nostrils. His hair was a thick, black rag clinging to his scalp. As he took slow, deep breaths, I could see his ribs against his skin. Veins along his arms were blue and purple threads that led across each hand to long, dirty nails. The nails of his pinkie fingers were unusually sharp. Was he homeless? A gang member? Someone's boyfriend or husband who messed around one too many times? Maybe he was an addict who owed money or got high on someone else's supply.

My mother was not witness to any of this. "Where can we take you? Are you okay?" she asked sweetly.

Swollen lips with half the skin torn from the bottom formed a smile as he leaned forward. He placed one pinkie fingernail to her neck. It was a pointed spear that threatened to open her vein. It was sharp enough to do so. Her body went rigid when he pressed it into her skin. "Drive to the Guadalupe River."

My chest hurt from the violent thumping of my heart. I didn't know what to do. My mother was trying to be a good Samaritan and this was her reward. Was he even a man?

I didn't want to die, not like that. I tried to think of things in the car to use as a weapon. There was nothing. It was the car of a single, working mother. My mother cried silently as she drove. Her lips tried to muffle sobs as he moved closer to the back of her seat. He was breathing in her hair and down her neck. It was at that moment I knew it was us or him. I would have to find some way to kill this thing in the car.

It was dark when we pulled up to the isolated area designated for people to park before they made their way to the river with their inner tubes and coolers.

"Good. Now get out. You two will be perfect. I've never used one so young."

The way he looked at me with his one red eye made my entire body roil. It was the same look a counselor at the Christian camp had given me the previous year. The tone in his voice was the same as when the counselor would brush up close to tell me what he thought of my body. My breasts were barely buds and legs just twigs poking from denim shorts. I wanted to cry and scream and ask God for help. The only thing that kept the counselor away was a boy who I liked. We were going around without anything physical happening, yet we were at each other's sides whenever possible. The counselor would ask what this boy was doing to me when no one was looking. I hadn't even kissed a boy by that time. I was too ashamed to tell anyone about the counselor. When I returned home, I refused to go back to camp or to church.

Now, on the edge of this park there was no boyfriend, husband, God or father. For both my mother and me, all the men in our lives had fled. But we would find a way.

He leaned in closer, over the front seat, and licked my mother's neck with his bloody tongue, which looked like a parasite-infected snail as it throbbed and writhed against her skin.

"Not my daughter. Please, not her. Do whatever you want to me. Just let her go."

I could see he was aroused by her pleas and fear. There was something else I noticed. On the back of his neck there was a wound. It wasn't big but it looked like it might hurt. I unbuckled my seat belt slowly, with trembling hands. When his red eye shifted to me to drink in my terror, I jabbed my fingers as deep as I could into the wound behind his neck. I dug into his flesh as if trying to pull out his spine. The sound of his ripping skin and screams filled the car then shattered the windows. I took the opportunity to use my other hand to dig deeper, pull harder. My mom fumbled with her seat belt before biting the arm that was pulling my hair. He let go of me, but I refused to let go of him.

"Mom, pull!" I screamed.

She twisted to her knees to face the backseat. With both hands she pulled on the loosening skin at the base of his skull. Black liquid oozed and spurted from the gaping wound, hitting me in the face. He continued to roar, shouting curses in languages we didn't understand. The flesh was falling from his back, revealing another layer of skin. It was gray and rubbery like that of a dolphin, only darker. His skin was sloughing off in our hands until he jerked back, causing it to tear down to just above his chest.

It was a horror with a smooth scalp and features of a human. The eyes were the same, yellow teeth the same, only more prominent as it had no lips. It grabbed both of my mother's arms, digging its nails into her skin. I jumped to the backseat to try to release its grip. I continued to pull at the flaps of skin but with little effect. It barely noticed this time. We had revealed its grotesque nature. There was no reason to hide any longer. As my mother and the thing struggled in a flesh tug of war, a thought popped into my mind: the man with the belt around his knuckles.

I removed my bra, which clipped in the front, twisting the arm straps around both hands until they felt secure. I wrapped it around the thing's neck until the muscles in my arms ached and the elastic straps cut off my circulation. It gasped for air and clutched its neck, releasing my mother. As she stumbled back, she pulled a layer of its brown flesh down to its waist. The ribs that protruded were thick ridges that surrounded a concave chest. Its heart beat ferociously inside. Its hands were scratching at my hands and forearms, trying to force me to let go of my bra garrote. I screamed out in a pain unrivaled to this day, but I would not let go.

My mother readjusted her position to bring one snake-skinned boot over the back of the seat. With all her strength, she aimed straight for the middle of the creature's chest.

Its heart stopped beating and its body went limp as her boot broke through the sternum. We were both covered in black goo and blood when its chest exploded. There was no explaining this to the police. If this shit didn't come off, we couldn't afford another car. We dragged the body out of the backseat to the side of the river, the safest place to light a fire. There were always matches or a lighter in the glove compartment because my father was a daily weed smoker to the day my mother kicked him out. We would use those to burn the body. The mound of flesh was hesitant to catch fire at first, but it soon blazed in the night. We walked away, feeling satisfied it was dead.

The drive home was silent. There was nothing to say.

*　　*　　*

The little house we shared with my grandfather was full of light, which was odd at that time. Mercedes would be worried. We walked through the door, hoping no one would notice our torn clothing, messed-up hair and bloodied bodies. The priest sat at the dining table with Mercedes, a candle with Christ holding a lamb burned between them. Mercedes gasped and crossed herself and ran to my aid. The priest smiled and nodded, making sure to make eye contact with both of us. Without a word he blew out the candle and left.

We both have scars from that night, but we earned those battle wounds. We survived. Don't ask us what it was because we don't know. The priest tells us it's something that doesn't concern us; we should just be proud we defeated it.

If I learned anything from my youth, it's that I'm always ready for a fight.

MAL DE OJO

My mother said I was a really cute baby that resembled a little orangutan with untamed, spiky strands of red hair and big brown eyes, always looking for food or someone to carry me around. People would stop her on the street or in the supermarket to tell her what a beautiful baby she had. Of course, you must always touch someone or something you admire, otherwise bad things might happen to that person or object. With children, it usually comes in the form of illness.

I think I was just over one year old when I had a bad case of chicken pox. My mother took me to the doctor, but they dismissed it as another childhood illness that needed to run its course. She waited and waited, but I wasn't getting better. Days and nights were filled with my screams. Nothing would ease my pain or her distress. This had to be the doing of an unseen hand.

Finally, my mother decided to seek help. She would have someone perform the Ojo ritual. A woman named Olga came to the house with fresh eggs from her backyard and candles. My exhausted mother allowed her to inspect me.

"She looks very ill. Let's see what's happening."

I lay on our bed fidgeting, trying to pull off the socks tied to my hands to prevent me from scratching my already badly blistered skin raw. To this day I still have scars.

The candle with the sacred heart of Jesus was lit. The two women prayed over me while Olga rubbed the egg the length of my body. I forgot about my itchy skin and wanted the egg. I continued to reach for it. My mother went to restrain me, which caused me to shriek so loud it scared both women. I kicked and wailed violently, causing Olga to drop the egg. It splattered upon impact. The yolk was a gooey red mess of blood. My mother and Olga had to cross themselves when they saw that the shape of the contents of the egg resembled a person.

"Someone wasn't admiring your daughter. They were cursing her."

But who would curse us? My mother had been through so much in her young life, becoming pregnant while still a teen, and now a curse on her baby. What would anyone gain by cursing a baby?

But there were more pressing matters than a curse by someone unknown. After paying Olga, my mother didn't have much left for food. We would go to the store to get what little we could afford.

My mother looked at the amount she owed for the groceries, then scanned the pile for what we could do without. She told the woman to put the bread and butter back. Grandma Carrie always had lard and flour at her house. We would eat tortillas; no need for bread.

The cashier gave my mother a repulsed look. "If you didn't have enough why did you bring this stuff up? Now I have to call a manager. Can't you count? I'm surprised you aren't paying with food stamps." It dawned on my mother that this was the source of the curse. Every time she shopped here, this same woman always gave us a dirty look.

"Touch my baby."

The woman gave her a disgusted expression. "I'm not touching your baby. I barely want to touch your money."

Through gritted teeth my mother repeated herself. "Touch my baby."

She grabbed the woman's hand and ran it across my crusty, calamine lotion-spotted arm. Without buying anything, she stormed out of the shop. That night she cried over my crib praying for this illness to go away and to have the strength to carry on to achieve something in this life. She had dreams, too.

The following day the fridge was still empty. She would have to go back and face the woman. But she noticed something as she lay in bed. I wasn't crying. She peered into my crib to see the rash fading and me breathing rhythmically instead of making a ragged, whistling sound. When I awoke and drank a full bottle of milk, my first in a week, we returned to the market. The woman was gone. What a relief. At the checkout a young man wordlessly scanned the groceries. We had just enough without the bread and butter.

"What happened to the usual cashier?" my mother asked.

"Oh yeah, she called in sick. Think she has shingles and it sounds pretty bad."

My mother looked at me, smiling and playing with a toy in the shopping cart.

We don't know where that woman is, or what she is doing, but my mother became an attorney in her forties and all her children are happy, with college degrees. You can't curse blessings.

THE MOST WONDERFUL
TIME OF THE YEAR

I'm trying to cook dinner while listening for the washing machine to finish, with one eye on my eldest to make sure he's still at the table doing his homework. My little one, only four years old, is begging for a snack. I try to explain, for the tenth time, that dinner will be ready shortly. His incessant demands never seem to end and the begging with fat tears in his eyes are enough to make me want to run out of the house with nothing but my phone and the clothes on my back. I wish I was talking about a romance gone wrong, but this is motherhood. There is no way out and no breakup. I can't ghost my own kids, as much as I want to at times. The big one is like Nosferatu, lurking around the house, shuffling from the kitchen for feeding back to the lair of the playroom to play the PS4 with his friends online. There is a permanent scowl on his face from me badgering him to shower, do homework or chores around the house. God forbid he helps his beleaguered mother.

The baby, bless, with her sweet face, is like a Siamese twin attached to my chest. Her wails are as painful as a separation without anesthetic when I try to put her down even to make a cup of coffee. Our relationship is like something from that B movie *Basket Case*.

The middle child has an angel's face with the disposition of Damien. All three so very different, but in the end I'm like the nanny in *The Omen* that hangs herself from the front of the house and screams "It's all for you, Damien!" Then all goes dark when my neck breaks as I forget any of my needs because it is indeed all for them.

The fun of Halloween has ended and now its's time to get down to the business of Christmas. The middle child *needs* the new PJ Mask life-size talking action figure. If I didn't think it would scar him for life, I'd show him *Child's Play*. Maybe he would stop asking.

The eldest is happy with cash or video games. The baby just wants to be held; plus she has a playroom full of hand-me-down toys. There are so many toys my house resembles the aftermath of a tsunami of wood and plastic. There are multiple wakes strewn across the floor. The middle child is old enough now to want everything and anything he sees. He understands the concept of new things. To this I say: fuck all the adverts snuck in between cartoons showing my kid the new and wonderous toys available to him. As soon as I hear the advert jingle float into the kitchen, my sentry post, I know I have to stop whatever I'm doing and watch for the millionth time. The sheer greed on his face makes me want to toss a pan at the TV so it's forever broken, but without TV or an iPad my husband and I might never have sex again.

These days I can't seem to keep up with any of them. And now it's that dreaded month we have to ensure is 24/7 magic. The month of December is one long concert, play, home-baking, exam-taking, house-decorating, card-writing, gift-buying frenzy. Every weekend is jam-packed with events that are mostly enjoyable for children. No wonder most people love Christmas as kids. As an adult there is no longer that anticipation of what could be under the wrapping. Adult toys (not to be mistaken for the bedroom kind. Those are a year-round gift anyway) are bigger and more expensive. The adults in the family choose what we want ahead of time and pick names from a hat for gift exchange. It's very civilized, but not exciting, kind of like going from dating to married with kids.

Thank the heavens and hell one of my girlfriends has organized our very own women-only Christmas party.

This night out is a long time in the making with our conflicting schedules. All of us women gather like a coven at a restaurant or bar. It could be a public toilet, as long as there's booze and it's devoid of husbands or children. We just want to commiserate, get drunk, laugh and remember there is a world that spins beyond middle-age duty. Unlike when we were in our twenties, there is no attention from the opposite sex. Half of us don't wear makeup and the others have just enough energy to fuck our husbands or masturbate. Nobody has time to fuck someone new.

The evening is fun, with most of the women wanting to leave when I feel like I'm just getting started. Begrudgingly, I say my goodbyes. There is still enough time to catch that last train.

The wet cement underneath the heel of my boot is a wonderful sound. It's a city sound unlike the buzzer of the dryer or the clinking of dishes in the dishwasher. I feel like I could be twenty-five again walking home from a date that wasn't half bad. Since I live in the suburbs, the trains don't run at frequent intervals. I have a bit of time to kill. I walk slow, relishing every second alone. As I make my way to the station, a single shop is still open, which is odd. Then again, Christmas hours I suppose. *Why the hell not?*, I think. It's a bookstore. Just to be sure, I set the alarm on my phone to alert me when I absolutely must leave before my carriage turns back into a pumpkin.

Candles flicker and fill the shop with the faint scent of pine and cinnamon. There's no one at the front desk. I look around, thinking of all the books I want to read, but the only stories in my head are those of mischievous trains or masked pajama-clad heroes.

There's a bin of free books. I look at my phone: still enough time for a quick look through. There is an unmarked red book with intricate calligraphy and symbols. The alarm goes off. I have to make this last train. Without thinking, I slip the book into my handbag.

When I arrive home my husband is sound asleep with the iPad still propped on his belly as his video game plays on. I slip into bed, hoping to get a good night's sleep before a wonderful morning of rugby training in the freezing cold for the eldest, followed by a five-year old's birthday party. Tomorrow I will be teeming with bags of joy and good will to man.

I wake up before everyone on a mission to get my Christmas shopping done online and we head out the door for rugby training that morning. What the fuck was I thinking, leaving my Christmas shopping until the first weekend of December? That stupid life-size action figure doll thing is sold out everywhere except eBay, where assholes are trying to flog it for hundreds of pounds. I don't think so. I'm sure it will all be fine, and we can find something else.

After standing in a wet blanket of drizzle and fog during rugby, we rush home for the birthday party. It's two hours of my life I will never regain as I feign interest in talking about my kids even more than I do at home with my husband. These parties are usually at eleven a.m., so too early to drink for most and we all drive. Like I said, wasted fucking time.

The looped Christmas music and mince pie over watery coffee make me want to vomit or sit down. I'm feeling a bit woozy. Nothing a bottle of red wine won't cure later tonight. Right now, I just need to make it through. The small birthday boy unwraps his last present. It's that fucking stupid doll I can't stop hearing about. Immediately my child runs to my legs and starts begging. I will do anything to stop that noise that tells me I'm a failure at this parenting thing. My ears prick as the mother whispers she bought it months ago. That smug look on her face burns me inside like a lighter igniting plastic. All my frustration begins to melt and turn into tears.

I lock myself into the bathroom and cry. I curse the day I decided to have children, I curse my youthful stupid belief in love and family and all those hooks that keep us tethered to earth, but infect us at the same time with something no tetanus shot can prevent. I reach into my bag for tissues and makeup. The other mothers will probably know this fresh coat of paint is from stifled sobs, but we don't have to talk about that. This is what we chose, and motherhood is such a wonderful thing, like Christmas.

My fingers find the mini pack of tissues, but there is something else: the book. If my husband can sit in the toilet for hours with a book, why can't I?

My black mascara tears soil the pages; my guilt and sorrow throb from my heart like a little beast trying to rip through. As I fumble around, something unexpected causes me to stop feeling so damn sorry for myself. On chapter four a naked woman lounges back while a demon's head rests between her legs. Underneath it reads, 'A spell for those hidden desires. Call my name and I shall answer.'

I scoff and read the words of some mumbo jumbo incantation out loud. When it comes to the point where you speak your desire, I say the first thing on my mind. I want that damn doll so my kid will shut the fuck up and give me peace. I just want a nice Christmas where everyone is happy. I want to feel like I'm doing okay because this is the only job I have. There is always the sense I'm not doing enough. There are tears in my eyes and the words of the spell are soaked with black blots of mascara. At the bottom of the page in small writing, like parenthood, there is a warning. "Any spirit conjured will be there for good. They can only leave of their own volition." This makes me snort. Take my damn soul while you're at it because I think it's as shriveled as my breasts from nursing three children.

My husband interrupts my moment.

"The kids are getting restless. Are you okay? We need you." I look in the mirror at my streaked face. It's unrecognizable to the point that there could be anyone in my place. They don't really need *me*.

I mentioned it's Christmas, and of course the party gave me a party bag that keeps on giving – a bad stomach bug. But Mama can't be sick. I go between school concerts and school runs shivering and dripping in a cold sweat that makes me look like I'm transitioning into some beast. The aching in my bowels is worse than any period pain Satan himself could conjure. I grit my teeth and smile through it all. But not all is lost. One of the mothers has told me about a small shop in Surrey that might have that toy I need before Christmas. I'm willing to sit in my own shit if it means putting an end to this chase.

I drive for forty-five minutes in the rain to get there. Seeing the shop devoid of people makes my heart sing. Maybe there is a chance.

The woman at the till is young and completely uninterested in customer service. I can tell by the way she remains staring at her phone as I walk in.

"Hi, I'm looking for the PJ Mask life-size action doll. I heard you might have one."

She looks at me in disgust as if I have interrupted something so important it might alter her life forever. I know I look like a wet jaundiced mermaid from hell, but just do your damn job.

"Sorry, all sold out."

My stomach cramps. A little voice whispers in my head, "She's lying. It's in the back. Just wait." At first it startles me, but then I feel grateful someone, anyone is on my side for once.

I force a smile and pretend to browse the aisles. When I see the young woman busy with another customer I wander to the back. The place is small enough I doubt they have CCTV, but I look around anyway. Nothing. I'm trying to be as quiet as possible in my frantic search. The place is a disorganized mess. I wonder what they pay kids these days. Out of the corner of my eye I see the doll. It's underneath a puffer coat but there is no mistaking the colors of the masked hero. Then a voice stops me.

"What are you doing here?" It's the damn girl.

My hands begin to shake. I can see them wrapped around her throat as I throttle her against the wall for ignoring me, for being pretty and thin and young without any effort whatsoever. She probably spends hours bitching to her friends how fat she is. God, I want to murder her just for being her. There is a growl inside of me. Is it my belly awash with virus or something else?

"I thought you said you didn't have one," I snap.

"That's mine, so technically we don't. But I will sell it to you for two hundred pounds. Cash." Her smile is a smear of bright red across her face.

The voice in my head is back. "What are you going to do about it? If you want it, take it. I'm here to help."

Without thinking, I feel my fingers ball into a fist as they reach for a cricket bat I scarcely remember noticing. In one swift arc of my arm I hit her across the face, splitting open her lip. There is a calm that comes over me. The stomach pains are gone, my fear and worry about everything being so damn perfect, including myself, is no longer a thought.

A little voice growls just above a whisper. "It's so easy to get what you want. Just take it. I'm here now and you have nothing to worry about. Look to your left. There's a box cutter. Use it. Watch all her youth spill out of her throat. Step into her blood and complete the spell. I promise you'll be everything she is and so much more. I'll always be by your side. Inside of you."

I feel myself smiling as I watch her fall to the ground. She hits the floor either dead or unconscious. I feel my empty hand begin to reach for the box cutter, but looking at a face that is hardly out of the teens softens me. I drop the cricket bat. Suddenly, the cross I wear around my neck feels tight, like it's choking me. My left hand tries to pull it off while my right pushes it back to my chest, helping me. I will myself to kneel next to her. Is she dead? Thank the heavens she's not. Just out cold with a nasty bruise and cut. With all my anger stewing inside, I grab the doll and run out the back door.

The cold air stings my eyes and lungs. The cramps have returned.

That voice hisses, "Why are you fighting? You called for me. You wanted this. Now I'm here to stay. Don't you want me to make all your wishes come true? What about that man you have a crush on? I bet you'd like a night alone. I can do this, but you must let me live inside of you. Let me use your hands as my own. 'Tis a small price. Stop fighting."

I remember the book, my desperation at that party. I didn't think it was real, but it was. *How the fuck is this real?* My thoughts of the girl are gone and now the only things that concern me are my husband and children. Will this thing come for them next? Will I do something I can't take back? What if that cricket bat was the box cutter? This thing has to go. It's ironic: children have a way of bringing the worst out of you. However, it's at these times you must be at your best. They are the best part of me that will live on.

I rush back home with this doll next to me, thinking back to my own childhood. When did we fall into the anarchy of needing it all? I pull over to a charity shop with the doll in hand. The woman's eyes are wide as she watches me approach the till. Without saying a word, I leave it on the counter and shove a fifty-pound note inside the collection point for a relief effort in a part of the world that will never know basic needs I have every day without thought. She thanks me, and I smile, trying to hold back tears and shit that is threatening to pass through me. Claws are digging deep, I can feel it. It's no longer the virus at work.

The voice hisses, "You are so weak. After what I've done?"

I ignore it. Maybe I deserve this thing inside of me to forever torment me for being a Grinch with a heart too small.

My next stop is to a food bank. I unload all of my groceries still in the back of the car and hand them to a vicar.

He shakes my hand. "Bless you!"

The voice sounds weaker. "Stop this! This is not the plan!" My stomach hurts again to the point I feel I might shit myself. I don't care. Sweat is running down my back and between my breasts. I must look like hell. I don't care. I have just enough vision to make it home where I will have to face off with this demon.

I run into the house and run straight for the toilet. Behind me are my family's voices.

"Where are the groceries? Did you remember the nice mince pies? You okay?"

After ten minutes I feel so much lighter. I look into the mirror as I wash my hands and see a shadow across my face.

The thing is right behind my eyes, its voice fainter than my baby's breath. "This isn't over. The spell wasn't completed but that doesn't mean I won't return."

I turn on the shower and lock the door before anyone has a chance to intrude.

As I enter the kitchen my husband is giving me an incredulous look. "Where were you? Did you get the thing?"

I grab his glass of wine from his hand and open the computer. Without giving anyone notice, I open the supermarket website and order a complete Christmas meal that should be delivered just in time.

It's Christmas day. The house is a jovial din of chaos. The baby is crying, and the two boys are fighting over what Christmas movie to watch. The middle one didn't even notice there is no action figure this year because he was too busy trying to reclaim his old toys that his sister now enjoys. No one is dying because I didn't make everything from scratch three days ahead of time.

The demon is long gone, perhaps, and must have tired of me not really giving a shit. I sit in the middle of everyone in my pajamas stained with baby food and drink my champagne straight from the bottle. Fuck perfection, my demons, the other demons residing in wait. It's Christmas after all.

PENTAGRAM PEEP SHOW

No one needs a soul in this godless place.

The front of the house is lined with framed vintage horror and adult film posters from the 1970s and 80s, the glory days of porn. Big bushes, soft bodies and natural, uneven-sized tits. Blacula casts his sexy gaze upon all that enter. From the bar lit with multi-colored lava lamps, you can order a maximum of three drinks, because drunks can't come and that's what you're here for. Don't worry, performance anxiety is normal, and it will fade with a single mouth-to-mouth kiss. When our tongues meet, every desire hidden beneath the trap doors of your heart open to me, spread wide like inviting legs.

You wait at the bar. Shelves of liquor are attached to a glass case of skulls tightly packed next to each other. Eyes open, mouths clenched in a thirsty grimace. A single bartender serves drinks or offers edibles baked with enough THC to give you a slight high. Put away your money because it's no good here. We deal in the currency of blood and desire. Your name will be called on a speaker that cracks with static. On the hardwood floor you follow arrows painted in gold leading away from the bar. Continue through an archway until you reach a wall of doors. Above each one, a round light blinks red or green. You must enter the one that switches to green. The rest are occupied.

Here at the Pentagram Peep Show you'll get the fuck of your life for the small price of your soul. Under the red glow of lights, you can view others slip in and out of the ecstasy of heresy on a round bed in the center of a revolving stage. Their eyes glaze over until they are as black as a bloodstain. No sign of life will ever escape. Some might be put off because taking pleasure in promiscuity is the surest path to hell.

Men and women sign away eternity for their dreams. I like both; flesh is flesh. The roundness of a woman's body is as delectable as the fresh oyster that lives between her legs. My lips on her lips while my tongue teases the pearl beneath the hood that causes her to shiver in my arms.

I will ride you fast and hard, feeling you about to crack inside. Hands grip my thighs while my nipples brush against your face. Almost there now. You scream "Jesus" just as your knuckles go white and your soul crumbles to ash. The tiny flakes float from your body into my mouth; manna that fills me. You are all mine now, forever and always. The next time you see me is after your death because your soul belongs to me. In a small room, within the infinite maze of hell, you will spend eternity watching others venture into my peep show. Some shout and claw at their hearts that it's not worth it, while others watch in evil delight, knowing the torment that awaits.

Like I said, no one needs a soul in this godless place. I found that out the moment I tumbled through the atmosphere in a fireball of light. My head crashed against a rock; my virgin wings dissolved from the sun. My nakedness shocked humans as they gathered around to see what would emerge from the small crater created by my body. Some tried to grab me with a lecherous look in their eyes, others threw stones. It was only by the kindness of a woman by a well that I found shelter. She covered my body with the garment that had been draped around her head. I spurted grit as my mouth and tongue felt dry from dirt. Her wooden ladle and bucket of water washed my throat clean so I might try to speak in a manner she could understand. With one arm around my trembling shoulder she guided me back to her hut. She looked at me with pity, deep sorrow as she wiped the blood from my cut forehead, dabbed my singed back that emitted black eddies of smoke where wings once attached. The pain of her touch caused me to wince, and salt water leaked from my eyes. Blood coated my thighs from my draining body. How strange I would bleed from there.

"You have been cast down as a woman. Whatever did you do?"

I didn't understand her words until she sent me on my way in the world.

"Demon. Fallen angel. Brown temptress," I heard behind my back. I sucked my first soul from a goat herder who tried to make me his third wife.

There isn't enough time to tell you how I ended up in Amsterdam. The blisters, the beds, the souls I reaped. How does anyone end up where they are? But here I am. The canals that lead to the red-light district are beautiful in spring. Tulips burst with color along cobbled streets. People on bikes ride peacefully by. Not far from my establishment of ill repute, you can visit the last home of Anne Frank. Every year I leave an offering. It reminds me why I do what I do and why I led the revolt against God. My back spasms where giant iridescent wings once sprouted as I cram my human body into the small spaces of the home turned museum. When I leave, I look to the sky as blue as God's left eye and curse him once more.

"One day," I whisper, "I will suck the glory from you until your eyes roll behind your head."

With my hands in my pockets in a multicultural modern city, no one bothers me anymore. I slip into the unassuming brick building built in 1780, though the foundation is much older than that. All those Flemish painters who rose to fame passed through my doors. Rock stars, artists, writers, all the same. I killed a few Nazis in my day, luring them with entertainment. They expected a cabaret of local women and instead stared into the eyes of a horde of demons.

I sent my most pale, Rebecca, to offer the group of German soldiers an invitation to our show.

"Bring the officers," she giggled, making sure to lick her lips, flick her blonde hair and give them a wink. Her hips swayed from side to side as she walked away.

Back then, the property looked like many of the older buildings, significantly smaller and narrow. Besides the bar in the main salon, it looked like a brothel. Candlelight on elegant candelabras illuminated the rooms. Bottles of champagne and whiskey greeted the cabal of soldiers expecting a jolly good time. We passed out cigarettes without care for rationing.

"Where is this show we've been promised?" said a sweaty officer with his jacket and shirt opened to the belly. Enough room for his guts to spill out, his breath heavy with cigar smoke and brandy.

I emerged from the top of the staircase, in gestapo boots and a short satin robe, bright lipstick glowing against my dusty, clay-colored skin. His eyes widened as the rest of us followed behind. Some were darker than me, their skin like molten lava, charred from free fall with the whites of their eyes glowing with malice. With every step, streaks of red cracked open then closed again. So beautiful as smoke rose from their bodies. Others had scales, and some had jagged teeth and beaks. You remember the painter Bosch?

The soldiers raised their guns but were disarmed in seconds by the others, who had been entertaining them for hours. The highest-ranking officer could not stand to face me as two of my fallen ones held him down with a single hand on each of his shoulders. Without their weapons and words of hate, they were nothing.

"All of you will die for this!" he spat.

I straddled his lap then cradled his face in my hands, my grip too strong for him to turn away.

"No, it's you who will die. Eventually all that you stand for."

Our wet lips carried pestilence to invade their cells as they attempted to invade the world. Boots stolen from Nazis we killed on the streets held them down by their necks while we watched them thrash in agony. The pestilence liquified them from the inside out. A small token, only a drop in the bucket that sloshed with all the evil in the world. Their bodies we burned, but their skulls we kept. They line the wall behind my bar with their souls trapped inside to forever watch the world turn without them in it. When the world ends, and it will, they will forever be locked inside the bodies of those they tormented, experiencing real hell for eternity. I consider them trophies and proof I must exist in this form.

I bet you never believed the Morning Star could be a woman, offering you things the other will not. But now it's showtime, not for me, but for my daughter, the one wrongly named the Antichrist. It is a proud moment to see your child become elected to the Senate of the United States of America. All of this planned from my humble business called the Pentagram Peep Show.

Showtime.

THE COLD SEASON

1

Tiny human bodies floated in their warm, amniotic-like fluid, dreaming away about nothing, while my cloned body grew inside a young Mexican woman named Juana. The only thing separating Juana and me were time, marriage and an angel's coin toss deciding which border we would be born behind. Would we be Mexican or Mexican American?

As I watched the incubation tanks, I couldn't help but become excited about my impending mind transference. No more mistakes, bad judgment or second guessing, because I would have lived one life before. Goodbye age spots, incontinence and back pain. My new birth was already paid and signed for. It's a slow process to ensure enough brain activity is triggered in my old body to be copied, uploaded to a computer then inserted into my newborn clone. When the procedure is complete, the heart in my old body will be stopped.

All I had to do now was wait.

Instead of incubation, I chose a natural birth, because what would God think of these incubation tanks? I chose Juana because she wanted a better life. As opportunities for some continued to expand, the opportunities for a large portion of the population were contracting. Humans were being automated out of the work force, making flesh the only resource for some.

My guardians, Marissa and Penelope, eagerly awaited their new child: me. After a few failed rounds of IVF and out of cash, they turned to this new industry created by Erin Goring, great

granddaughter of the great Elias Goring. We were the first
pioneers of mind transference. By agreeing to care for me during
childhood, they would have a baby and enough money for more
IVF or an incubation tank for a biological child.

Originally, I wanted one of my three children to look after
me, but they all declined. How soon they forgot all the years
I sacrificed at home to cater to their developing lives, which
would hopefully surpass my own accomplishments. I never had
the opportunity to go to college.

At least my son was honest enough to look me in the eye and
say, "Mom, I love you, but I always envisioned looking after you
as a nice, frail old lady my children would call Abuelita. Now,
you want me to take you into our home as a playmate for my
kids and give you the opportunity to throw spaghetti in my face
when you don't want to eat your dinner? No thanks."

Marissa and Penelope would be my guardians.

Today, I was having my final checkup before heading to the
warmth of Mexico for the transference. I was still youngish, but
I wanted my mind to be fully intact. It was imperative I saw a
doctor because this year I couldn't shake off a brutal cold. Every
year, I received a flu shot and did everything recommended to
avoid illness, but every year I had the same cold or flu. I guess
some mysteries of life were never meant to be solved.

For what seemed like months, my chest ached, causing my
head to ring with every cough. The general feeling of misery was
only matched by that of each of my three pregnancies. This old
body had long begun its process of decay and I was all too ready
to be rid of stretched skin, darkened enlarged areolas and joints
that creaked like the floorboards of my first home. Every year I
made the promise I would move from the east coast following
the great climate shift as the four seasons became too extreme
for me. I loathed the cold and the winters were now marked by
unpredictable vicious spells. The darkness was relentless, like the

peak of a virus replicating without mercy in my body. The mother in me couldn't bear to leave my children or grandchildren in case they needed me. I stayed in the cold, dark seasons for my family.

The doctor listened to my chest once, twice; took my pulse and temperature. He turned his back to me, took out his phone and sent a text to someone. God, was this cancer? Did he hear something so terrible he couldn't look me in the eye any longer? I was used to getting that from men at my age. When I was younger that never happened. Cosmetic surgery only kept me looking good until about sixty. After that I just gave up until this new breed of science emerged. Unfortunately, my dear late husband was taken from this earth before the procedure was perfected. Did I mention my late husband worked for the software company that invested in the mind transference technology? This left us a hefty nest egg that suddenly felt pointless. Who would I share it with? I prayed to God, hoping for a miracle, but my husband passed away peacefully post stroke, surrounded by those who loved him best. I would go into this experiment alone. For the first time in my adult life I was alone.

Even if we chose to never meet as born-again children or adults, it would have been a comfort to know he was out there somewhere. Our marriage had grown from instant attraction and sex whenever possible to discussing toilet habits when they were abnormal. Selfishly, I looked forward to sleeping with other people in my younger body without being unfaithful. I never betrayed him with my body, but I'd be lying if I said my thoughts didn't wander throughout the years when we weren't getting along or the same positions recycled yet again became routine. My love never wavered, only my physical needs.

"Mrs. Brancroft, you can get dressed now. I need to speak to my colleague. Can we get you tea or coffee?"

Tea or coffee. Really? If I'm dying I don't want to wait and I don't want any fucking warm beverages. I want the truth, my new body, and a bottle of champagne because babies and children aren't allowed to drink, dammit! But I can't say that. "No thank you. I'll wait."

The doctor returned after half an hour with a tablet. Erin Goring was on the screen. "Hello, Mrs. Brancroft. How are you feeling?"

I managed a smile and wanted to scream, "I feel like hell, bitch, with a blow torch on full blast down my throat and chest!" Those words just tumbled around my head and I said something I didn't mean.

"Oh, just fighting off a cold." I had to smile because that's the right thing to do in these situations.

She had a fake look of concern on her face. I didn't doubt a word from my mouth would go unheard, because she was concentrating on what she would say next.

"Okay, I won't draw this out. Seems like you have a rather nasty chest infection. At your age we're worried it could become pneumonia. If we wait we might miss your birth. We would have to start from scratch, or we could go to Mexico today and implant your consciousness into your clone in utero, then induce your surrogate or perform a C-section."

Wow, not what I was expecting at all. I hated pregnancy, so how would I take to being on the other side of the wall? Would this work? "What are your chances of success?"

Mrs. Goring looked uncomfortable and excited at the same time, with the wild look of an explorer finding El Dorado. "This would be the first in utero transference. Of course, we would reimburse you half the fee and cover any extra expenses, but the opportunity to see if this is possible is priceless. Imagine being able to tell us what it's like *inside*. Closer to home, but just as scary as space."

"Will this really work? What if I lose consciousness forever?"

A flash of worry in her eyes couldn't hide behind a perfect smile. "I have no answer for that. It's never been done."

At least she didn't bullshit me. I was tired. Tired of feeling sick with this damned cold and the creeping claw of age. My hearing in my left ear never fully recovered from the last infection. She said it herself, *at my age.*

"You need to be healthy enough for the procedure to be successful, meaning you won't die."

I didn't want to endure another cold season or birthday in this body. "I'll do it, but only if you give Juana the reimbursed portion of my fee and a resettlement pass if she wants one."

Abandoning politeness, Mrs. Goring slapped her desk. The smile returned. "I'll fly down and meet you in Mexico myself. Do you want your family there? What about your guardians?"

My family. My children. I loved them so and they were one of the reasons I was going through this strange process. The thought of the world turning while I could not partake in any of its delights brought on nauseating fear. I wanted to see every moment of their lives; despite the fact they now had their own lives. I'm sure my death would be a frantic disruption to their busy schedules. If it went well then it would be a pleasant surprise. If it didn't, they still had their own spouses and children for comfort. I'd be sitting on a cloud, explaining myself to Christ.

I didn't need to go home and pack a bag because my guardians already picked out tiny pink sleepers and booties for me. I'd be their baby for the time being.

My guardians were panicked when I called. They were afraid I had backed out of the procedure or something had happened to Juana, but when they learned they would begin their journey into parenthood, they screamed through the phone, forgetting I was there. It didn't matter much because my cough was getting worse, making it difficult to speak. Not long now; one way or another it would be gone.

*   *   *

The hospital was new and smelled sterile, unlike the world outside. Mexico was just recovering from the border wars with the US and the world trying to pull itself from global recession triggered by the trade and trash wars. You heard that right. We lost viable options of places to put humanity's garbage and it sparked a series of embargos. The Goring Corporation stepped in, for a hefty price, to shoot it all into space. There isn't a problem coin can't fix even if it means bankrupting governments that were on their last legs anyway.

My original plan was to check myself into one of the remaining resorts in Mexico selling rooms at coin-bottom prices with the lobster BBQs on the beach and bottomless margaritas. Plans don't often work out the way we anticipate. I was too sick and needed an empty stomach before the procedure. Here's to having another lifetime to indulge.

Juana was already at the hospital, looking nervous as hell, rubbing her belly while clutching a rosary.

I did my best to comfort her. "It's going to be okay. There's no risk to you."

She looked up at me with trepidation in her eyes. "I know, I just hope she will be okay. Putting needles and things inside of her. I've carried her, you, so long now. Sometimes I forget she's not mine." I liked Juana. She was honest and bright with a big heart. I hoped this opportunity would give her the boost she needed to make her dreams come true.

I gave her my ring, diamond crucifix and Cartier watch. My collection of jewelry and bags were saved for my daughter, but she wanted the new styles and didn't really care for 'vintage' no matter the worth. So my jewelry sat in a climate-controlled storage locker left unused. "Here, I don't need these anymore."

She gently pushed my hand away. "No, I can't. They told me about the extra money. Thank you. My family could really use it."

I told her to just hold on to my few possessions for me. It was she who was about to do something miraculous for me.

They were finally ready for us.

The room was cold, more than cold. My teeth chattered and body shook as I lay there waiting to be drugged. As the anesthesia kicked in, the cold invaded beneath my skin and traveled the length of my body. I imagined my blood turning into red icicles or those cheap foot-long popsicles wrapped in plastic that are meant for the hottest of days because it was easy to eat five at a time. My children loved those.

The surgeons began their checks and asked me what I wanted to listen to. There was only one song I could think of. It was the song that played during the birth of my last child. As the drugs passed from needle to spine, peace and warmth enveloped my body without a sniffle or cough to callously interrupt this moment. I could breathe and not feel the slightest of touches on any part of my body. It felt good to alleviate my body of what was causing my constant discomfort, like my previous C-sections. The thought of a new me was so exhilarating I almost forgot I could die. I was about to die. 'Seven Wonders' by Fleetwood Mac played in the background as my old life was extinguished.

Most of my adult life I'd been a caretaker, maker of brownies, chauffeur and boo boo kisser. Who would have thought I would be a pioneer for humankind?

This time around I would not have children, not because I didn't love mine. In fact I would die for all three without question. Love is all consuming and drowning, until your last breath leaves you, thinking, *Holy shit, my time is up. Where the hell did it go?* My children were not my mistakes. I was the mistake at the heart of it. I wasted time and life on things and people that really didn't matter.

Being childless felt like a new pathway with experiences once thwarted by the lovely but exhausting hamster wheel that is parenting. And if parenting can be a hamster wheel, then marriage is a Ferris wheel. One moment you're at the top with a breathtaking view, the next you're at the bottom again ready to jump off to find another ride. I might not even fall in love; just bed hop when the mood struck. My marriage was a happy one for the most part, but I found that just as exhausting as parenting at times. The constant compromise, the deal making. Even when you aren't trying, you find yourself seeking the other's approval. It hurts when you don't receive it. It hurt me to feel like my only place was in the home. Time ran out for me to get a degree and pursue a career once I had the money to do those things. My first rule in this new body was no sex in my young body until I was finished with college. God, that would wipe a whole slate of mistakes totally clean. Unlike the first roulette turn, I now had paper and coin. Everything was planned out, from the schools I would attend to clubs I would belong to. My coin was safely invested so there would be enough to make my dreams come true now that I knew, the hard way, how to play the game.

It was time to count backwards until I woke up in Juana's womb.

2

During one of our many family getaways I booked myself into a spa that had the most luxurious steam rooms and walkways that rained hot water on your back as you ventured room to room. You moved naked from one experience to the other until you reached the end of the journey with a door that opened to a darkened sauna smelling of herbs and flowers. Soothing music lulled your muscles and mind into total relaxation as you lay on a wooden bed molded to fit the shape of a body. I rested in a gentle twilight of sleep as long as I could while my husband played some muddy outdoor game with the children far away.

My memory was interrupted by a sudden jostling. My eyes snapped open. This wasn't the steam room and I couldn't smell jasmine. The amniotic fluid was everywhere and nowhere as it was part of me. There were voices beyond the flesh wall that I couldn't understand. Then it dawned on me. It worked. I was awake and aware and an unborn baby ready to start all over again in this world that would have cast me aside as nature intended if I lived any longer. I was still here so God must not oppose such an action no matter how controversial.

I didn't want to stay here. It was strange, scary and tight. I couldn't move without kicking or punching poor Juana. I could feel myself panicking as my heart picked up pace. The desire to be out was as overwhelming as the time I wanted to pull out my last child during the final trimester. *Shit! Stop it!* Irregular heartbeat in an unborn baby means trouble. *Stop it! Stop it!* I kept shouting in my mind. The voices were louder. The walls were tightening around me, tugging me, dragging me from this water cave I'd mistaken for a spa.

The lights were now on and I wanted to shout, "I'm alive, I'm here. Stop tugging and wrap me up. I'm fucking cold!" But only that little baby meow scream could be heard. I almost forgot – I'm an infant.

I couldn't clearly see them or speak to them, but I knew they looked me over, making sure I was okay with all my toes and fingers. Madam Goring must have been popping the bubbly, but how would they know I was there; that it really worked? I wanted to see my old body, which would be frozen in the event someone in my family needed a slice of me for survival.

They placed me in Juana's arms. She smelled wonderful. Hunger pangs made me wince. That stupid cold had left me without an appetite and now I wanted it all. She tried to put me to her breast but that's not what I wanted. I liked rare steaks when they were available, barbacoa breakfast tacos, gooey brie on crusty bread, red wine and sushi. *Don't make me drink that stuff! I know it's not 'stuff'; it's colostrum and it's good for me. But yuck!*

Unable to resist her hand or my hunger, I found myself drinking anyway. I'd tasted breast milk before, my own, but now this warm vanilla milkshake made me feel sleepy, comfortable. I was passed hand to hand, warm then cold, and prodded. The scientists, Marissa and Penelope, were probably all fighting for the chance to cuddle me, study me. All I wanted to do was sleep or eat. Strange not to have a single responsibility or worry. No one to lunch with, no buying groceries or homework to look over. I just had to lie there and grow, grow until my body fit my mind. Maybe I hadn't thought this through. That was going to be a very long time, and I'm bored very easily.

★   ★   ★

We must have returned to the US at some point, because I couldn't smell Juana's milk anymore and I was given the store-bought stuff. Still yuck. How much longer until they weaned me?

I think the baby years went by okay from the photos I've seen and the stories I've been told. Marissa and Penelope were always smiling and ran to me when I cried. I tried to form words but I couldn't, and the more I tried the more wailing rang between my ears. Being a baby was harder than it looked. I loved my children as babies, especially newborns. They were adorable little things that didn't move and only wanted my arms. Then something happened and they went from Mogwai to Gremlin, making it known how much of a failure I was at this parenting thing. From what Marissa and Penelope told me later, I skipped the Gremlin stage, opting to do as I was told, including eating vegetables.

You would think I would remember everything, but the brain is easily overloaded. Studies showed that the short-term and long-term memory sometimes dumped information. With a little tweak you could choose. I chose short term as a child because I didn't need to remember watching cartoons or going on a walk to feed ducks. I wanted to remember all the things I wanted to change when I reached of age.

3

I know it's harsh to call a child of twelve a little bitch, but she was. As a parent I knew it wasn't her fault. Her parents were probably a real pair of assholes, too tired, busy or lazy to say "No," so they raised another little entitled asshole.

It was lunchtime when I spotted the pigtailed brat making fun of a girl with scuffed shoes and a packed lunch. I wouldn't stand for my children being bullied so I wouldn't stand for it now.

"Hey! Yeah, you, leave her alone. What's your problem?"

The girl stared me down with her pigtailed posse in tow. Her little eyes narrowed, looking me up and down, trying to formulate a put-down to impress the gathering crowd. The great thing about age is that you forget what it means to be insecure. I was ready for the insults. What could she possibly say that I hadn't heard before? Sticks and stones.

"Don't talk to me, fat ass. *On scholarship.*"

I waited for more. Something, anything juicy. That was it. *Really, that's all you got?* Where I came from a scholarship was fucking amazing. I badgered my children night and day to work hard for scholarships. Before my brain had time to think like a tween, I felt venom and daggers gather in my throat ready to stab and burn this wicked little bully.

"Bitch, please," I said, "take your scrawny ass back into class and leave me and everyone else the fuck alone. You aren't better than me or anyone else and if I catch you acting like a trifling little cunt again, I will beat your ass and cut your hair off your head until you look like a zombie."

The circle was quiet. I realized I had spoken to a child in a way I would never tolerate. I wanted to put all my words back into my mouth as soon as they were out.

With quivering lips and eyes full of tears, she ran off without any of her companions. Shit. Marissa and Penelope were gonna be pissed. As the kids scattered, one boy hung around the bike stand staring at me like I was an alien hiding out in someone else's skin. I had seen him before. Like me, he kept mostly to himself, always finishing the assignments first and all around didn't quite fit in. We stared at each other for a moment before he hopped on his bike and left.

Penelope and Marissa were a little upset when they had to leave work to meet with the headmaster of the school. He didn't want to hear any of it, especially since the parents paid good money to send their kids there. His reputation, blah blah, so on and so forth. The school only accepted me because they received a hefty grant from the government for accepting mind-transference kids. The parents of non-transferred kids were not aware of our presence for our safety and privacy.

When the little bully and her parents arrived, I couldn't help but notice her smug face matched her mother's. That explained it all. When confronted about her mistreatment of the other girls, she tried to pretend it was all one big joke and she was *so* sorry. It didn't take long for my guardians to take my side once the mother gave us a pity smile, saying, "Well, we understand it can't be easy in your family. I mean, it's not the traditional way. You're both women."

I half expected Penelope to jump out of her chair and take off her earrings, ready to throw down. She just shook her head.

Penelope spent the entire car ride home venting. "Really, we can clone humans, transplant said humans, yet we can't cure ignorance. What a world we live in. Bunch of cunts."

"*Thank you!*" I shouted.

"Hey, little lady, you aren't off the hook yet. I know you're a woman inside a kid's body but just try to rein it in a bit. Okay?" Marissa said this with a wink, so I knew I wasn't in trouble. Maybe a little babysitting duty which I could do. I should have kept my mouth shut and cut the girl's hair in class instead. The do-over thing doesn't account for your nature. That doesn't seem to change.

★   ★   ★

I sat alone at lunch, watching my peers, when the strange boy on the bike after the fight approached me.

"I'm Sam. You're one of us, aren't you?"

How the hell did this kid sniff me out? Only one way and that was because he was one, too.

"My name is Araceli. And I'm one of what?"

He sat down next to me and pulled out a cigarette. "Please, I've been watching you and it's like looking in a mirror. We both have that bored all-knowing look you only have when you've lived a lot of life. Plus, I'm on the board of the company."

This kid was no kid. "Okay, tell me more."

He held the cigarette in front of me. "Wanna smoke?"

I pushed his hand away. "Absolutely not! I'm doing it all over and I don't want cancer or bad skin. This is my second chance. Why do you think I'm at this fancy school? Isn't that the entire purpose of mind transference? Besides, you'll get us in trouble and I've already had some trouble. Put that thing away."

His floppy hair fell over his face and I could see he would be pretty handsome in a few years. "Nah. I'm a trustee of the school. I can do what I want. You know, I had a really good life. Money, family, kids, a few wives. I just wasn't ready to die. Who you with?"

I had to know who this kid was. "Got guardians. My kids

wanted no part of it. I see them occasionally, but their children find it too weird."

"Yeah, I'm with my son. He hates it, but I said if he didn't take me in there would be no inheritance. And I want to know what's happening at the company. I'm Sam."

Sam Moreno was a decent kid. As a man years before, he ran a large banking fortune, one of the few that survived the global recession. One of the reasons he attended school was out of boredom. Kids are pretty limited with what they can do during the day. We started having lunch together on the days he decided to show up for school. We recounted our past lives and what we wanted for the future. At least I talked about what *I* wanted for my future. Sam just wanted to live again as he did before as a trust fund kid who would eventually be ushered into the same schools' internships and jobs. He would take his place on the board once again, having all his previous knowledge and experience.

After that day we were inseparable.

He didn't mind coming to my house for frozen pizza and soda while we watched *Scarface* or *The Godfather*. Marissa and Penelope were relieved I finally had a real friend instead of relying on them for constant companionship. I have to admit, it must have been creepy having a small child trying to hang out with you like old girlfriends meeting for brunch, giving you parental advice and cursing.

I certainly didn't mind going to his mansion to sneak sips of top-shelf whiskey and tequila. His son was never around so we had free rein of the house. To my surprise he shared my love and knowledge of 90s-00s rap and hip hop. Watching this kid with a cigarette hanging out of his mouth knowing the words to 'Let Me Ride' by Dr. Dre was a sight that left me in stitches.

One Sunday after Sam rolled us a particularly fat joint, he led me into his son's office. He flipped on the computer. I didn't know what I was looking at, but the faces scared me.

"These guys changed the game altogether. Until now only the rich and people of extraordinary gifts had undergone the procedure, at least that's what we were told. No problems, few deaths, everyone happy to be in an exact copy of their previous body sans any genetic abnormalities. Well, these are the worst of the worst according to society. Their damaged minds have been implanted into different bodies and placed in a compound that resembles a quiet gated community with all the things in life that should make for a well-adjusted human. This is where Goring Corp. began.

"Originally, this started as an experiment to see if rehabilitation is truly achievable or if damaged goods are only good for recycling. These guys were throw-away humans no one cared about. They barely cared about themselves. Most of them have been executed or locked away again for crime, but a few survive, living out their lives in that gated suburb. Goring took over the project when the government ran out of money. That company had all the government's money after the trash wars. Now, this new technology is everything. Talk about unethical business. Feel bad if it ever leaked to the public."

I didn't know what to think. This heavy shit was a buzzkill. You only read about this kind of weird experimental stuff. It didn't really exist.

"Why are you telling me this?"

Sam continued to scroll through the photos of inmates. "Don't know. I'm bored. I've got no one to call friends anymore. All my so-called friends can't exactly drag a twelve-year-old around. My son has his life and his wife still talks to me like I'm her father-in-law. Is it just me or does this part of the program suck?"

It did kind of suck. Childhood was a holding pattern for us. I couldn't wait until I was at least sixteen or seventeen and I could really start my do-over again. This time I would be prepared for all those standardized tests, interviews, pop quizzes, and the best tutors coin could buy. My dream of being a childless, unmarried travel writer would be mine no matter what and no one would tell me what I could or couldn't do.

That night was uncomfortable and hot. I couldn't stop thinking about the experiments. There was one in particular who stuck with me. He was a young vato with a shaved head and a teardrop at the corner of his eye with a large neck tattoo of something indecipherable. He looked savage, not because of his outward appearance, but something in his eyes told me things had gone terribly wrong through no fault of his own. He was a leading gang member with ties to a cartel down south. The government now recognized the cartel as a legitimate business because our government wouldn't tolerate violence and death pouring into the streets anymore. All those little shake-and-bake jobs in the country were closed down, and low-level dealing was shut down completely. It wasn't long until other countries followed suit. This guy got locked up for trying to renegotiate the terms of the cartel union of marijuana farmers. Someone didn't like him shaking things up, or more accurately making things fair. His imprisonment was a convenient reminder to keep your place in the order of things. He got too big for his boots, taking on something he wasn't seen as fit to run.

He reminded me of my brother, long gone now, who spent most of his adult life locked up, and was then stripped of the right to vote or purchase alcohol and monitored until he was six feet under. He was a kid tried as an adult who may or may not have perpetrated the crime. Since no one would fess up and everyone pointed fingers at everyone else, the entire gang of boys got sent away for the maximum sentence. Problem solved.

I tossed again in my bed, thinking of my children and the privilege they were afforded. My daughter beamed in her two-carat diamond earrings upon graduating from the University of Pennsylvania with her big plans that we would never deny. My mamacita out-achieved me academically in my previous life, but isn't that an integral part of your job as a parent?

I cried myself to sleep, wanting my husband again and those sleepless nights with my newborns. Marissa and Penelope loved me and I loved them, but I felt so alone. Childhood seemed like a repeat of the shortest day of the year in winter.

4

The bar was dimly lit with people speaking to each other quietly. A stunning wine list and chilled-out house music created the perfect ambiance for meetings that might end in sex. There were still things in the world technology could not improve on. There was a reason Sam chose that bar. After I turned down his marriage proposal during college, we slowly lost touch. I finished my Ivy League education, loan-free from the money I had in trust from my pervious life, then landed my dream job as a travel writer for a top magazine. I had my own travel show exploring what was left of the world's treasures. It was a solitary life of business-class champagne dreams. With my youth restored, I slept with whatever man I wanted, not shying away from making the first move. How often I fantasized about this when my marriage hit the twenty-year mark, and now I was living it. I had the wisdom and confidence to stay away from the toxic relationships that marred the youth of my previous life.

There was also no better time to travel. The old ways of the world were changing fast. People were sick of hunger, violence, food and energy shortages, threats of war and extremism. Bankrupt governments made way for companies to broker deals of peace where everyone was a winner. Countries existed only in name, but it was their contribution to global survival that mattered. Being on the brink of extinction woke everyone the fuck up. No one would survive if there wasn't a world to live in and with the promise of making death an outdated notion, there was a hell of a lot of living to do. There was the Middle Eastern Coop, the People's Republic of Textile and Pharmacology Conglomerate, the Continent of Africa Solar Energy Company, the Affiliation of Destinations of Leisure, the European Union (part deux) and of course the Tech and Research Cartel of South American Countries. The promise of financial prosperity and technological advancement for everyone made the most vicious lay down their weapons for a slice of the pie. For the first time, humans moved around a world of softened borders with ease. We traded in some paper, but mostly in coin (aka *ElectroCoin*). The world was big and beautiful, and I got to see it all without being pulled out of bed by demands for breakfast or cartoons at an hour meant for returning home after a great night out.

Sam was living his same life, only bigger. From the word go, he had made more coin in his ruthless reign as CEO of Moreno Banking and Insurance. And the world, with its unpredictable climate, needed lots of insuring. Scientists tried to predict if we would suddenly become a greenhouse or a freezer in desperate need of defrosting. Only time would tell, and this fear was exploited.

Perhaps I missed something when we were apart, because his ambition was greater than before. The company had become aggressive in its takeovers and wild expansion into scientific unknown. Next to India, Mexico now housed the largest tech research hubs, thanks to Sam. The Cartel were masters of security, so Sam relocated all the research facilities there. He trailblazed with a 'Don't come for me unless I send for you' attitude.

Goring Corporation's clone reinsertion was now widely accepted and available on credit if you passed the psych evaluation. World leaders agreed to everything and anything for a promise of re-insertion, but if the board didn't like your politics, too bad for you. Better change them quick. Sam wasn't just a rainmaker; he was the monsoon and the typhoon that never ended.

The previous year I visited a resort tailored for the reborn that very few common folk could afford, but they all wanted to know about. Surrounded by the pristine mountains of Italy and Switzerland, people recounted their lives and shared secrets. It was sold as a place where you would meet like minds and feel at home in a world that could be isolating for the select few. Truth be told, it was nothing but fucking and deal brokering.

I waited for Sam at the bar, not knowing what to expect. Maybe I'd sleep with him tonight for old time's sake. He walked in with a blue suit, crisp white shirt and no tie. He looked great.

"Hello, old friend. Thanks for making time for me," I said.

He leaned close and kissed my cheek. "Anything for the woman who turned me down."

The evening was drink after drink until in our drunkenness we decided to make our way to Nobu for all-you-can-eat sushi. Somewhere between the sashimi platter and another carafe of sake, I remembered companionship. I could feel the hot flush of lust dragging me to the bottom of that little ceramic cup where I would drown. We had lost our virginity to each other all those years ago after I'd promised I would avoid sex until I completed my education, and now here I was with a heart tingling with something that resembled love. I missed him.

The soft blanket of being with someone who knows you best was what I was missing on my jet-lagged nights and dining for one in the best of restaurants that served rare ingredients. How lonely it was to look up without anyone to tell it tasted like dirty socks or you were currently experiencing a mouth orgasm. But this is what I wanted and yearned for in my previous life as I sat with baby vomit on one shoulder and an infant on the other, while my other children fought over who got to sit at the right side of me at the dinner table.

For years I tried to push away thoughts of family and marriage. I even steered clear of the 'good guys' who reminded me of my late husband. It was too painful to think we could have been in this together if only he could have held on for another year. I traveled far and wide, but in the end, loneliness always found me.

Sam and I walked out of the restaurant, laughing about the day of the pigtailed bully. I didn't know it, but Sam had been one of her targets. Being a gentleman and all, he didn't dare fight back.

All at once he kissed me deeply, grabbing my ass the way he knew I liked. "I have a surprise for you." He pulled out a freshly rolled joint and suddenly we were teens again.

I followed him, barely able to walk in my heels. Eventually he ripped them off of my feet, smirking. "You can replace those. You won't need them tonight."

Not a few blocks from the restaurant he led me into a hot basement with wall-to-wall people. To my pleasure and surprise there was an actual human DJ behind the decks working the vibe of the crowd. Sam knew I loved dancing and wanted to do more of it in this lifetime. The last time I enjoyed a night of sweaty salsa was when I visited the newly organized Confederate States of South America. It was a small place in the middle of the budding jungle. The world was dumping money in reforestation because as long as humans were still on Earth there would be no hope if we couldn't breathe. It was a privilege to stay in the village and report on the lives of those who had a place to call home.

Ozuna remixes pounded my chest and it was time to dance. Sam was invisible to the crowd with no one recognizing him. He threw off his jacket, caring little for the sweat stains that ringed his armpits. He knew I didn't care as long as he was close. Our bodies were synchronised to the Latin beat, the thick smoke in the air making it hard to breathe. Tonight, we would go home together and I would ask him to stay as long as he wanted. The sex was familiar yet new, allowing us to ask for what we needed to get off, but our bodies responded with the excitement as if it were the first time. Sex is best when they know what it takes to make you come.

The second time Sam proposed I accepted. By this time, only one of my children wanted to go through the procedure that was now only done in utero, even though Sam had secured places for all my children and grandchildren. Without hesitation I allowed myself to become pregnant. I wanted that feeling of life kicking the shit out of my bladder. Life was great, but life doesn't like or respect our wants or needs. Whoever said life's a bitch should have said life's a fickle bitch.

★   ★   ★

My husband and best friend since we were twelve was not who I thought he was. They do say natural born leaders are one life away from natural born killers. All day he had been acting cagey, mumbling to himself. Whenever he saw our child, he turned away with a dark shadow overcasting his eyes. I allowed him to go through whatever was plaguing him, believing it to be work-related.

While our new baby slept soundly with the night nurse, I pulled Sam aside. I poured us each a glass of our favorite champagne to hopefully loosen him up. "Drink this and tell me what's going on. I know you well enough to know this is big."

He took the champagne flute and drank half of it all at once.

"I've been wanting to tell you this for years, but I didn't want to lose you. You're one of my other halves."

I didn't like how he phrased that. "Go on."

"Remember when we were kids I showed you some classified files? Prisoners."

I sipped on my champagne, mulling over memories. "I guess. It was strange. I remember not sleeping well that night. Why?"

"I know I approached you as Sam, and part of me is, but I'm also Angel Gomez."

My mind didn't know how to react to this lightning bolt. It was a moment that left me too stunned to speak.

He took another drink and continued. "Sam approached me in prison after I signed up for the experiments. He said he liked how I ran the cartel, unionized the marijuana farmers, and my negotiating skills, but it was small time compared to what he had in mind. He couldn't believe the balls I had to stand up to the government when they tried to undercut the cartel and farmers. He needed a modern Machiavelli. You see, Sam Moreno had been diagnosed with early onset Alzheimer's disease. Doctors couldn't give him any definitive answers on what could or would happen long term to his transferred consciousness. The science wasn't there yet. So he made the decision to give himself a Plan B. He would transfer *two* conscious minds. A best friend he would grow up with like a brother from birth. The second consciousness would keep him going if he should falter. If all went well, when this body was about to die then he would be on his own again. He had been fucked over in business too many times to trust anyone on the outside of his own mind. We would grow up together in one body, making decisions together."

My head spun from the information dump and champagne that I'd drunk without tasting. "You're one of those men in the files he showed me *and* the real Sam?"

"Yes, but I think Sam died a long time ago. When I was about twenty. I'm sorry. Every time I tried to tell you I could only imagine losing you."

"Tell me about you, Angel."

"I told him to fuck off at first. But he came to visit every week, sent me commissary and books. He even got the warden to loosen my restrictions. When he offered me a chance to live *his* life, I said okay. But there was a catch. He would be coming along too. At least the small part that still existed. There was a chance I'd go batshit loco with two voices in one body, but I thought it was worth the risk. I had nothing but time, looking at four small walls for the rest of my life for fighting for myself and my people. Now, I could be in charge, rich as fuck and pulling off one hell of a coup when the time was right. Best part was he wanted me to reach out to the cartel and secure funding for even more research. The cartel loved the idea of going legit across the border. The womb and genetic modification business was the future. Together we could be the future."

I could feel tears streaming down my face. My mind didn't fall in love; my heart did, but I loved a half truth. I couldn't blame him. The same drive that made people risk their lives crossing rivers and seas and Juana renting her womb to me drove a criminal to find salvation in another's skin. Sam was desperate not to fade away. A huge sacrifice for a chance, a chance at this life. I took the same chance transferring my consciousness in utero rather than the tried-and-tested postbirth method. Desperation birthed us, united us. I drank and poured more champagne.

"You want to leave me now?" He had tears in his eyes.

For once I didn't know what I wanted. I'd just had a baby, something I'd promised I would never do the second time around. I could feel my hormones surging, causing my breasts to leak and giving me the uncontrollable urge to cry or become irritated at the slightest thing. What I did know was that I loved this creation that was my husband. He had achieved things no one thought possible from a single man. Well, not completely a single man. My husband was the man Forbes called the greatest business genius of our time and the times to come: a homie from the streets. His name was Angel.

"Is there anything else you need to tell me? Any shady business deals that could drag our family through the mud or you away in handcuffs?"

He passed me the bottle of champagne. "No, babe, I'm one-hundred-percent legit. Sam made me promise to give up anything that would compromise the company. All he wanted was my street expertise and not really giving a fuck. And I didn't. I didn't care what those rich folks with their degrees and who they knew thought about me. I wanted to get things done and make our name big. I did just that. And he let me have you. A homegirl at heart. Where else was I going to find a woman like you? He was my companion in my mind, but you were the companion in my soul. That's why I waited. I didn't want some cold woman wanting me just for my money or name. Since we were twelve you were the only one. After I saw you put that chick in her place, I knew."

Hormones and champagne bubbled through me, resulting in sobs I couldn't stop. I don't even know why I was crying like I did all those years ago as a baby, unable to speak but wanting to be heard. Unable to find the words my mouth had yet to learn to form. At least unlike those baby years I hadn't shit myself – yet. I was ride-or-die. I had to be since death was no longer an option.

"Who else knows?" I took another gulp and I could feel the bottle was nearly finished.

"You and the surgeons, who are all retired on some island with the promise of a free mind transfer."

I didn't want to think what the fallout would be if anyone found out who Sam really was. Could the world handle a seeming outcast from the wrong side of the border being the globe's greatest influencer? Would people feel conned? There were wolves at the door waiting for this opportunity to pounce and rip him to pieces along with all that he had done. I would keep and protect this secret.

"One other thing." Both his hands were on my thighs as if I would need steadying after another revelation.

Great, what was it now? I wasn't sure how much more I could take, and it would mean opening another bottle of something to get me through this night.

"When the time comes, I won't be cloned as Sam. I'll be Angel."

I remembered the tattooed guy in the files he had shown me when we were twelve. "And when people ask you why you've come back a different person than before?"

He gave me that smile he liked to give me before slipping his hands down the back of my pajama pants.

"I'll tell them to mind their own fucking business."

Sam was my Angel.

5

To say the Goring family was not happy with the takeover was an understatement. The leaked files made headlines, sending many of the family members on permanent vacation. When Mrs. Goring was reinserted into her clone, Sam decided to make his move. All the grubby secrets the Goring dynasty had acquired over the years were exposed. If there hadn't been so many security breaches in the valuable technology that was mind transference, no one would have followed him. It was only the threat of losing the greatest scientific achievement humankind had seen that made any of it possible. Sam brought in the cartel bosses to secure the research facility.

★　　★　　★

Sam tossed the phone across the room. This was not good. Many years had passed since we took over Goring. I assumed the threat had passed. It had not. Jack Goring was on the move, having grown tired of beach life and caring for his mother, now a child.

We had to dig deep into the past to mitigate the problem. In fact, the world was devolving into a feudal system of conglomerates anyway, so why not go back to the tried-and-tested maneuver of marriage to quietly tuck away a problem? We would unite the Goring clan with our own through my daughter. Everyone loves a royal wedding, a baby, a fairy tale of what could be if given enough time. There would be a lottery inviting ordinary citizens to the celebration.

"Mom, I don't want to marry the guy."

I hated myself for having this conversation. We were supposed to be beyond all of this. "Mija, what else are you going to do? You have as many lifetimes as you wish to accomplish so many things. But now we need this. Our family needs this."

"You mean Dad needs this."

The fewer people who knew the truth of Sam and Angel occupying the same body the better, but my beautifully stubborn daughter would not budge unless I told her. I wished there was some other way. I was asking her to marry and hopefully have children to carry on our empire, and when Sam and I were ready she would need to ensure we were safe and hidden until we were at least twelve again. One terrible reality of the mind transference was the rate of infanticide among those in positions of influence. Sam already had a plan in place for us.

The following week my daughter, Mariella Alcazar, would announce her engagement to Jack Goring. Everyone said it was a good match as they were young and eligible, making their names around the globe, Jack in business and Mariella in physics. Her body was of earth but her mind always in the stars. I had no doubt, my daughter would take humans beyond Mars.

★   ★   ★

The village was deep in the Sonora Mountains in Mexico. Sam had begun building this compound for some time. The hacienda smelled familiar, like home.

Then my heart seized with a feeling of calm, soothing my trepidation. A woman who reminded me of Juana emerged I looked into her eyes and knew we would be safe. She wore the diamond crucifix I gave Juana all those years ago.

"What are you doing here? How did you…?"

Sam's hand was on my back. "I found Juana and gave her another lifetime. No one will find us here while we're children. Then we'll re-emerge into society, taking our places again, my love."

We were both seventy years old and ready to retire. I lay next to Sam on the operating table, our age-spotted hands clutching onto each other. Selena belted out 'Tu Solo Tu' as a single surgeon and one nurse began the procedure. As the song played on, I could feel myself falling into a warm, drowsy, tipsy bathwater that would extinguish my life. His fingertips began to slip through my own as we would die and be birthed back into this world again – together. Juana was carrying twins, my husband and me.

I mouthed "I love you" and he responded with "Te amo."

Life is a beautiful, wonderful thing and I am so grateful to experience it all over again. One lifetime is not enough. I hope these notes I leave behind will continue to remind and inspire me to always live my best life until the end of time.

THE LATIN QUEENS OF MICTLAN

They were called the Latin Kings on Earth, but we are gathered here as the Latin Queens, the leaders of Mictlan while the gods are away. You can see from my exposed, flayed chest that I no longer have a heart. There is only a black mass, half congealed blood and half obsidian, in the space where it should be. One half is my anger, the other is my sadness, and deep within there is just enough love left for another lifetime. Obsidian is the very thing my ancestors used when splitting open their captives to appease the gods. As Queens of Mictlan, our teeth and nails are sharpened spearheads of this sacred black rock. We have nothing to offer the gods, but ourselves. Down here, that is enough. From collarbone to the waist we are laid bare; this is how you know one of us approaches. There is no hiding what we are made of anymore. Down here, shadow is like daylight.

Inside I'm as dead and dark as the oceans. Once they teemed with life that sustained others, but now there is nothing. There is only so much ache a heart can feel in a lifetime, and perhaps that is why mine turned half stone. My touch and tongue are hot if you share my bed; my bite will shred your flesh within seconds if you come too close or threaten any of my brothers or sisters.

I'm the leader of the Queens because I don't fuck with the trolls and poisonous creatures that scurry around at night looking for easy prey. You can find them in their tattered clothes, stinking of excrement as they slink in and out of garbage heaps, sucking on the bones of the recently dead or their victims. Some we trap then release into the wilds beyond the realm of Mictlan, never to be seen again. The dangerous ones we dispatch with mercy because even though half of our hearts are volcanic stone we are not without the concept of charity. But do not take my lenience for weakness. There are waterfalls of blood for the thirsty to drink from or sit by and listen to the calming babble as they remember their lives and loved ones.

The source of such beauty is the hanging bodies of those trying to disrupt what we want to accomplish during our time here. We are building on a kingdom pleasing to the gods so one day we might return to Earth. One chance is all we have. Unlike in life, I know exactly what I want and there is nothing to keep me from achieving it. I have like-minded Queens – their souls cry out to me through this cavernous place as the sound of my conch shell reverberates to signal a new cycle would begin. My guard dogs, half the size of a man, with fangs of a grizzly, patrol the nine realms on gold leashes held by my loyal Queens keeping the order of things until the day the gods return.

We are a crew of ride-or-die mujeres making the best of our nightmares, running the levels of Mictlan with the bravado of politicians of the twenty-first century and raking in the profit like those Fortune 500 companies of old. Here, the currency is blood, flesh and piety. In the center of the village square I have erected a fountain that stands ten feet tall made from loose teeth gathered by the orphaned children – it grows by the day because in return they are guaranteed safety and love that not all were afforded in life. It also keeps them out of trouble. Here you may pull out one of your own to toss into the clear water and make known your wishes for a second chance or prayers to find a loved one.

There are all manner of humans lurking in the dark of Mictlan since the world evaporated in a flash of disease. The ones responsible will be found sooner or later, and when they are, we will have a parade through the multilevel world of Mictlan with screams and gritos that will sound like music to the ears of those who seek answers or vengeance. The perpetrators of great crimes must not be allowed to return when the time comes to rise again. History must not repeat itself. Filth will not be dragged back down to Earth again.

What I am today has been years in the making.

★　★　★

My weekly shopping was always done in the early hours of the morning when my three children and husband were still asleep and I could get in and out of the supermarket with ease. Just as they rose from their beds ready to announce their hunger, everything would be put away except what I might need to prepare breakfast. That Saturday morning, I was driving home when I heard a loud pop, followed by the entire car quaking with me inside.

My first thought was I had a flat tire. I struggled to gain control of the car until the sky lit with the brightness of three sunsets for a matter of seconds, then died back down. There was mist settling over the neighborhood that couldn't be fog – more like an aerosol can had been sprayed from the heavens. I braked in the middle of the empty road, trying to understand what was happening as car alarms and house alarms wailed around me. It took me a second to notice I didn't hear any dogs barking. The sky returned to the natural morning light and I continued home in a sneezing fit.

When I got home, I put the groceries away and waited for the family to rise. My skin itched. Nothing but silence. I went to my eldest child's room first, the teen who was always hungry. I opened the door and screamed for all the times I regretted giving up my freedom for chicken nuggets and back talk. I pulled out tufts of my loosening hair, thinking of all the times I wished away years because the moments trying to cope with small children and my hidden ambitions were too difficult for my brain or heart to process. In my shame, I fell to my knees, thinking of how rotten I was in all ways that mattered. Guilt hardened around my bones like arthritis. I could feel something taking over me. When I opened the second bedroom door, I vomited on the floor. I didn't have the heart to cross the threshold to see what I already knew.

Still alive with everyone dead, I wondered if this was my punishment for wanting to be alone when the chaos of family life overwhelmed me. All three of my babies were gone. To this day I mourn them, but for my husband of twelve years I couldn't muster a tear. It wasn't that I didn't love him, but he wasn't part of my body. I told you I was a heartless beast.

Seated at the foot of our bed, I looked at his corpse, thinking about the last fight we had. I hated how small he sometimes made me feel, like my only value was to keep him and the children happy. I thought of the small digs that made me feel guilty for wanting more. The blame was squarely on me for giving in to my fear of failure and taking the easy road of meekness, allowing myself to submit to everyone and everything except my dreams.

The last fight left me sobbing alone in the dark with a bottle of wine between my legs. Here I was again, crying, another bottle of wine between my legs, but this time because they were all gone.

I was next. My naturally brown skin was ashen, with pink pustules cropping up minute by minute – my nausea, which rivaled morning sickness during my pregnancies, was ceaseless. The only way I kept it at bay was the alcohol and leftover weed my husband's friend from college had left in our garden shed for when he stopped by for a visit. I hadn't smoked since my twenties. If I was going to die, I might as well enjoy my last hours. I was alone, sick, and to make matters so much worse, blood leaked from between my legs because I was pregnant again, or had been. My husband didn't know. I was afraid to tell him, not because he wouldn't want another child, but I was unsure and scared. It would mean many more years of not pursuing my dreams. Soon they would be gone forever.

I would have to endure this the way I endured a miscarriage during one of my children's birthday parties. Before the forty guests arrived, I awoke to the worst backache of my life. When I sat on the toilet, the seat felt wet beneath my thighs. My legs were covered in dark brown and bright red streaks of blood. I cried for an hour, leaning against my bathroom sink until I realized I had to get up and begin preparing food for the party. The bouncy castle had already arrived and there would be no disappointing a three-year-old. I allowed myself to continue to miscarry while the party carried on. I bled until my tears dried inside and today would be the same, except I would bleed until I died and there was no need to smile for anyone.

I inhaled deep from the joint until my chest ached, then released a plume of smoke into the air. A cloud floated around my head as I took a big swig of red wine to wet my dry mouth. I felt good in my haze as I hoped to black out from this nightmare. Whatever popped in the atmosphere killed my family and was now killing me. I sat on my living room sofa, smoking, drinking, and listening to 90s rap as loud as the speakers in my home would permit. Cypress Hill's 'Ain't Goin' Out Like That' bounced against the walls, reminding me of the days of teased bangs and lip liner a darker shade than the lipstick. High and dying, I thought of the decisions that took me from barrio girl to go-go dancing my way through college, to a job, then housewife. In my life I navigated through so many levels of hardship and worry; at least my death would be on a high instead of a middle-age slump. I was going to be as high as the fucking Milky Way and whatever else was out there looking down on us without mercy.

During 'Crossroads' by Bone Thugs-N-Harmony, I prepared for my funeral, putting on all my jewelry and makeup. At my feet I placed my favorite tubes of lipstick, a photo album, and a notebook of the plays I wrote in my free time that would never see the light of day, plays about my barrio days with cholas I called friends and the others who surrounded me after school to kick my ass. I laughed at the cousin I was jealous of, because her mom made her money shoplifting, so she always had nice clothes, while my single mom struggled as a social worker. There were all the people we lived with because we didn't have our own place. There were the pregnant girls and the women raising their babies alone. There were the gangs I barely escaped. I only had my mother to thank for her vigilance and sacrifices. She taught me about sacrifice. I thought one day my children would learn the same lesson, to navigate a world that loved no one, certainly not the world as it was shaping up to be. Before it all ended, democracy around the world was slashed and burned like the forests that would soon be non-existent and the seas that were hardening like plastic.

We all thought it would be nuclear warfare, not germ warfare, that would be the end of us. I don't think the perpetrators anticipated the virus would take on a life of its own the way it did. Some things in life have no masters. Humans weren't masters of anything. Fuck, we could barely master our own desires and instincts. I closed my eyes, thinking of the births of my children, the only real accomplishments in my life, and went to sleep.

*   *   *

I awoke in a tiled and stone room. It appeared to be a circular throne room surrounded by waterfalls that trickled in an uneven flow. In the center, nine steps of neatly stacked skulls and bones in the shape of a pyramid were topped by a throne made of bone. The armrests and back were ornately carved in the shape of different animals. My chest hurt, like I had inhaled and held on to smoke too long or just emerged from a coughing fit. That was when I looked down to see I no longer had a chest. My entire torso was bone and muscle. Exposed ribs encased my lungs and ribbons of muscle and veins. Just to the left was the space that should have been my heart. Half of it shone like a hard thing in the flickering of the torches that lined the room; the other half looked sticky, wet and misshapen. I took one of my fingers – now capped with black nails that resembled arrowheads, the edges uneven, yet sharp – and tapped my heart gently to figure out what sat in my chest.

"Welcome, my child."

I jumped. There was a figure, a man. "What the fuck? Am I hallucinating? Am I dead?"

"You are indeed dead. I'm sorry."

There was only one thing I wanted to know. "My family?"

"They are here, on another level, perfectly safe. You can't see them, I'm afraid. At least not now."

He walked closer until I could get a clear view of him. He was a man of chiseled muscle standing seven feet tall with the eyes of a serpent set in a wide, bronzed, hairless face. His nose resembled a sharp beak that was pierced with a small bone. Upon closer inspection, I could see his skin was not smooth like a human's, but a sheet of small, brown scales. Behind him, the tips of two large, brightly colored wings – like those I imagined on an archangel – stood another two feet above his head. Thick, black hair hung in a single braid. A leather loincloth was the only clothing he wore. I'd be lying if I said I wasn't curious about what was beneath based on the rest of him. He was the most beautiful and alluring thing I had ever seen.

"Who are you and why do I look like this? Is this hell?"

He let out a laugh that echoed through the room. "My name is Quetzalcoatl. And Hell? Hell no, as you say down there! This is Mictlan. I have brought you here because a terrible calamity has befallen the Earth. All of humankind, including every beast, has perished. We knew things were terrible for the humans, but we never thought the end would be so swift."

If I had a real heart, I would have sworn it skipped a beat at that moment. I knew what happened was bad, but not end-of-the-world bad. "Why am I here?"

"Come with me." He offered me his feathered and scaled hand that felt cool and silky to the touch.

Behind the throne there was a stone altar. He picked up a mirror and held it to my face. My skin was bronzed, with a week-at-the-beach glow, eyes solid black and teeth sharp obsidian points – it was a gleaming grill that no rapper could rival. On a table next to the throne were my tubes of lipstick, photos, my plays and the gold jewelry I wore at my death.

"Thank you. You still haven't answered why I'm here."

"I may be a god, or I should say we may be gods here, but we can't be two places at once. The gods have united and will return to Earth to clean up the mess that has been made by mankind. This behavior cannot be tolerated; such gems are not deserving of being spoiled. It has been agreed Earth will be restored. But Mictlan is teeming with souls, more than we are used to accommodating, and those souls need rearing. Not all are good. The hideous nightmares that befell Earth have taken form here. You will be a Queen, keeping an eye on things while we are away. Once all the sin is consumed and a new cycle begins, a select few will be allowed to enter through cenote and cave back to the realm of Earth."

I didn't know what to say or think. Me? "I'm not good enough. I have no idea. I was just a mom. I'm sorry. I'll just fuck it up. I can't."

"You can and you will. Do you forget who you are? At your core." His finger tapped on the hard surface of my heart. "For forty years you were alive and in those forty years you endured trials and tribulations, yet came through the other side. You made choices in your youth, difficult ones that enabled you to survive, to grow. And you have imagination. You will need that imagination to harness the frightening things you will encounter. You need to believe and rise. Find others like you and harness their power."

I reached down and grabbed my earrings and lipstick as he continued to hold the mirror to my new face. I saw thick lips. My boys got those from me. Black eyes – my daughter would have had the same. My hair – which I refused to cut even though my husband constantly badgered me to do – remained smooth against my face and parted in the center. He then took a small conch shell from around his neck and placed it around mine.

"They will hear and heed your call. Share your resilient fires with each other. Each god has chosen a human to take the lead in each realm. I have chosen you. Let me show you."

We exited the throne room and stood at the top of a pyramid overlooking the surrounding area of Mictlan. Souls were everywhere, aimless and wailing, some tearing at each other while others fled some crime. Their amorphous forms swayed like a carpet of sea anemones with the tide. How would I accomplish this? I thought of all the failures, the dead world and the place that taught me more than most of my books, the streets. Life in my neighborhood, the legal and illegals I knew.

The importance of family. That is when I knew how I would organize this first realm.

I took the conch and blew as hard as my lungs would allow. The meandering souls stopped and looked in the direction of the noise. I wanted those who didn't have a chance on the other side, because the stakes are resurrection. They would not fail. I knew in my heart this was a test for mankind, how we fared in a place we couldn't control or think we own. You don't have to be a good test taker to rise to a challenge. And rise these women will.

That is how I became a Latin Queen of Mictlan.

TRUCK STOP

1

"You're so ugly. Did you know your mother was a jackal that left you to die after you were born? I wish she would have eaten you instead."

I didn't know if my mother was a jackal, but she must have fucked a demon or been abducted by aliens to produce me. I will never reproduce because I was born without a womb. That space is occupied by something I can't explain. Maybe that's why I was considered so repulsive.

At ten years old I was summoned to the head mother's office to discuss one of my wild drawings. Usually I would receive an odd look of dissatisfaction, the sister twisting the paper around to get a better idea of what was going on within my mind. However, I assume her patience with my oddity had worn thin like a threadbare sock with one too many toes poking through. I walked slowly through the halls that echoed my footfalls and the voices of the sisters teaching lessons. Rows of saints looked down on me in condemnation. What else could it be?

Before I could knock on the door left ajar, I heard conversation and a mention of my name.

One of the sisters spoke just above a whisper. "I was told her mother was found dead in the desert clutching a bundle and an empty jug of water. It was only because an immigration agent felt sorry for the infant that she ended up here. A dead mother with no sort of identification on her. How tragic. What would you do if you found a helpless little thing stuck between two worlds?"

"Yes. I heard that from the previous head mother, God rest her blessed soul. If she wanted the child here it must stay a secret. The officer took responsibility to file the necessary paperwork for a new birth certificate, giving the baby the name – Sonora, for the place she was found – the Sonoran Desert. No one believed she would live this long. The doctor who gave her a checkup at the hospital said she had a heart murmur, the sound an irregularity he had not heard before. Keep her comfortable for as long as possible, he said."

There was a pause I imagined they took to cross their bodies.

"Ironic that the desert and mountains found a small mercy to spare her but not her mother. God has so many mysteries. That's why we have our faith and our work is so important. She's still alive ten years later."

"I know, but the other children are spreading rumors the mother was a local prostitute. One had the audacity to say a jackal. The cruelty. Where do they learn such ugliness?"

Before they could say more, I knocked on the door. I held my tears and questions inside because I was not going to look for someone who no longer existed or mattered. Let them say what they wanted because I had the truth and I wasn't alone. And now I knew for certain my mother died for me. I held on to that belief more than God.

"Sonora, please sit down."

I sat in one of two chairs in front of a wooden desk with a Rolodex and phone. It was an old one with a twisty cable. Between two windows that allowed in the morning sun hung a picture of the Christ and his burning heart crowned with thorns bursting from his chest. Maybe I was made in his image, whatever he was. He stared back at me with soft blue dead eyes. I wondered if hearts could really catch fire.

"Sonora."

I snapped my head towards both women, smiling with the only emotion they possessed for me: pity. The head mother sat in the chair behind the desk and the younger one stood behind her. I looked down at my scuffed hand-me-down patent leather shoes that buckled across the foot. I loved those shoes because the buckle was in the shape of a flower.

"You're not in any trouble, but we are worried that you're having nightmares or are distressed in some way. This drawing is very scary."

I looked at the sheet of 8½ x 11 paper. A large mountain dominated the page with people drawn in crude backwards shapes crawling from a black hole at the top. Violent crayon streaks of red poured from the opening. I cannot remember if it was blood or lava. The drawing was a work from the mind of a child, which is often as mysterious as God. The shapes looked more like aliens or monsters than humans. At least they were smiling with wide grins and swirls for eyes.

"They aren't scary. And I sleep fine."

The women looked at each other, then back at me. I shrugged and swung my feet, which didn't reach the floor. The women continued to stare, and I knew they wouldn't stop until I gave an acceptable answer.

"It was something in my head. I don't know. I'm sorry." If in doubt, apologize. I believe that lesson was taught to me at the same time as the alphabet.

"Sonora, stop scratching your neck and chest like that! You will break the skin! If you don't want to be teased any longer, then act normal, even if you don't look normal." The young nun looked flushed with rage and disgust.

"Sister!" the older one snapped.

"I'm sorry. I don't know what to do with this child. She needs to know God expects us to help ourselves to a certain extent."

I looked down to see I had been clawing at myself this whole time. The flesh was bright red with nail marks that resembled the crimson slashes of my drawing. I brought my hands to my lap.

"I'm sorry. I won't do it again. I didn't notice. Honest."

They continued to stare at me hard, not knowing what to say or do with a child who was not their own and not wanted by anyone else. No one wanted to adopt me when I was a baby who had potential life-threatening problems, and when I was no longer a baby, I remained unwanted.

"You may go, but I don't want to see anything like this again. Do you understand?" The younger sister held the page up before tossing it in the empty metal garbage can.

I nodded sheepishly and walked through the quiet corridor back to my classroom.

As I sat down, the girl next to me mouthed, "Jackal."

If only I had been born with the teeth and disposition of a jackal, I would have gnawed my way through her neck so I wouldn't hear that lie again. If only I had swirly eyes and a ferocious smile like my drawing, there would be no more taunts.

Books and prayers. No TV. Three meals a day in a dining hall that always smelled like oatmeal no matter what was written on the white board hanging in the front of the cafeteria. At Easter and Christmas, we held a concert to raise money for us girls beyond what the local diocese contributed. Our uniform consisted of a white blouse and matching black skirt to the knee. There was structure without love, which was enough to get by until I turned eighteen and was expected to leave, unless I wanted to pursue a life devoted to the church. No thanks. All the emotions I am expected to feel I learned from Motown and Sister Bertie. When it was her turn for kitchen duty, the radio played very low. Songs about love, jealousy, hope and despair. When I was older, I realized she also hummed one of Motown's greatest records: 'Super Freak' by Rick James. None of the other sisters noticed. She swayed her wide hips back and forth, singing and chopping, giving me a wide genuine smile and a wink. There was no pity or malice. Sister Bertie and her music taught me how to navigate emotions we were expected not to show, emotions

I did not know how to understand or communicate because there was no one to experience them with.

The day arrived for me to leave the nuns. My actual birthday was never celebrated because no record had the exact date. The head mother provided me with a leather suitcase with double buckles, a bible, a package of cotton underwear, a simple white bra that didn't fit, two sets of spare clothes from the local Goodwill and a check for five hundred dollars left from the will of the officer who found me in the desert.

"Sonora."

How the sister had changed from the day she threw my artwork in the garbage. We were both women now. She could go and try to throw something of mine away. Her face sagged with dark double saddles beneath her eyes, the rest sallow and wrinkled like a crumpled piece of paper. I wonder how that felt.

"Tell me what you plan to do now that it's time to leave. You have no desire to stay here and devote yourself to God? He did save you. And since you cannot bear children, I thought this would be a fit for you."

My feet touched the ground and I stared at the simple white Keds I hoped to change for Dr. Martens or something with a heel, preferably patent leather. She stared at me, waiting for an answer. I had nothing to apologize for, but the words seemed like the appropriate response for my very existence. I had no desire to be a wife, no money for school, no real skills taught by the nuns except how to believe my rewards would be in heaven and not here on Earth. I would start in Tucson to find some means of work. I hated how she insinuated my only worth was to bear a cross for Christ or bear a child for a man.

"I'm sorry, Sister, that I don't feel compelled to stay. I have prayed about it. I guess I want to see the world."

"I understand. If you were called to be a bride of Christ, you would know. It's a beautiful feeling." She smiled and breathed in through her nose as if she was inhaling the fragrance of a bouquet of roses.

I mimicked her smile. "Thank you for your years of care."

We stood to face each other and shook hands. Her eyes searched mine, until they focused on my lower lip and neck. Her expression turned sour with pity.

"Good luck. I hope you find what you're looking for. You were a miracle, Sonora. Let God work through you no matter what you do. Allow your holiness to touch others."

Thank God she didn't burst into song, you know that one from the *The Sound of Music*? 'Climb Every Mountain'. God help me.

2

The first time, at twenty, was easy because the man had to be at least seventy-five, a regular at the big hotel cocktail bar where I waited tables for the past two years. Every time I refilled the little bowl with nuts and olives, his eyes would linger on me as he licked his lips then smiled with large white dentures. When he closed out his tab, he made a point to show off a wad of cash folded in a money clip when he left me a tip as big as his bill. One finger tapped on the cash like Morse code. After a few months he worked up the courage to invite me to his room. Instead of tapping on the cash, he brushed against my thigh.

"Would you grant a lovesick old man one last fantasy?" He placed the entire money clip in my hand.

I looked at the money, only half knowing what he might want. I didn't care. No immortal soul lived inside of me, because something else resided there.

The hairless mole between his legs was like a soft-boiled egg in my hands and mouth. No amount of stimulation could get him where he wanted to go. And I did my research.

The first time I watched a pornographic film began innocuously enough. The video store on the corner of my block was small with four rows of metal shelving in the middle of the floor and one wall lined with the same shelves. There was also a section dedicated to comics and magazines. It was run by a single proprietor who also served as cashier, Steve, who would glance up from his music magazine when I entered, shoot me a small smile then look away again. From the photos on the wall behind the counter, he'd met a few of the bands he read about. A stack of his reading material stood in the corner of the counter. Every time I entered he had a different horror film or music t-shirt on.

Typically, I bolted to the horror section to grab the new release before all the copies were taken. The horror covers made me feel like I browsed through a family photo album. In the horror section I found my place in the world, my home world. A place where ugliness didn't exist. All that was inside of each of us was shown on the outside without rough clothing from the neck to the ankles. No pretense.

As I stood there disappointed at no new releases, a man rushed past me, almost knocking into me. He didn't bother to look back or apologize, but I looked in the direction he came from. A green door with a handwritten note: *18 and Over. No XXXceptions.* What did that even mean? I thought I knew. A flutter in my chest. Bubbles tickling my jugular notch. My chin itched.

I kept hold of the horror film I wanted to watch, *Cat People*, as I approached the green door. Steve raised his eyebrows.

"You got ID?"

These were the first words he ever spoke to me. I nodded, rustled through my purse, and took it out with shaking hands. I felt a trembling beneath my panties, which wanted to be removed but I didn't know why. I allowed myself to look him in the eye for longer than a millisecond. Black eyes the same color as his thick head of hair that grazed his forehead. I wondered what the goatee around his mouth would feel like on my collarbone. Would I crack open at his touch? A tattoo of something I couldn't make out peeked from beneath the sleeve of his Lamb of God t-shirt.

He gave me his shy smile again. "I probably don't have to tell you this, but no funny business in there. I have a camera." He tapped on a screen hidden beneath the counter.

I opened the door. The lights were low, reminding me of walking into the chapel before dawn with only the glow of the candles lit the night before, melted to the nub, melted to a wet pool. There was no one else but me. I looked in awe at the covers that ranged from half nudity to a pile of bodies connected in ways that looked unnatural. How did they all fit? Soft moans came from a small TV overhead secured in a cage with the mouth of the VHS entrance uncovered, just like the crotchless panties some of the ladies on the back of the covers wore.

I had seen only flashes of skin on other bodies, keeping my own as covered as possible to hide from stares and ridicule. I brought one video close to my face, studying the sharpness of a red high heel and the line of the arch of the woman's foot. All the curves of her body were beautiful. I tucked it next to *Cat People*. I continued down the aisle, seeing masks, which frightened me a bit, so I skipped past. Older videos stood separately in their hard-yellowed VHS cases.

Steve's voice. "Can I help you?"

I backed against a wall of videos. I did need help. I needed him to place his hand beneath my panties and stop the little thing from screaming, whining to be soothed. Soothe it until it was quiet again. Did I find him attractive? That's a good question. Before that day I never noticed him. Didn't want to even though he was the first person to catch my eye in the shop. My fear of being seen was too strong. He stood in front of me, an offering. A tempting piece of fruit. I only remember the feeling of wanting his body. What did flesh taste like?

I opened my mouth to speak. Then closed it again. No way he would want me. I'm not pretty; I'm hideous, it's clear to see. My countenance belonged on a cover in the horror section once all of me was seen. I did not belong with these women with their long limbs spread open, the little pip between their legs acting as the control center to their being, giving out orders given the chance. Today I think how very sad it was that I saw myself that way.

"I'm sorry I've been in here so long. I'll take these two."

It was *Cat People* and one called *Rodeo* featuring an attractive couple. I liked the look of the woman with thick thighs and a round ass like mine. Her neon pink nails pressing into her brown skin. I liked she was the same color as me. A glossy mouth open, ready to tell and show you her secrets. The man next to her had his thumbs tucked at the waist of his jeans, pulling them down to reveal his hard body shining with oil. I needed to see how it worked. We were only told the anatomical facts, not the facts of life. And of course, all the scripture involving a man and a woman. Boring. I followed Steve out of the back room and to the cash desk.

As he handed me *Rodeo*, he smiled. "That's a decent one. It has a story and not that hardcore. One for the ladies. I'm Steve, by the way. You come in a lot, probably one of my best customers."

I couldn't look him in the eye again, feeling embarrassed. "Thank you. I'm Sonora."

The old man broke my memory as he rubbed himself while tracing his finger down the bottom of my lip. I could only think of Steve.

"I'm sorry, miss. Believe me when I say it isn't you. It doesn't seem to work anymore. Had to try. What happened to you? What is that on your face?"

I felt pity for him but tried not to show it. "I don't know. All I know is it might scare you."

"I seen it all, honey. Show me."

I pushed his spider-veined legs towards the center of the bed so I could sit more securely. I caressed my bottom lip, followed by my chin, with my forefinger. His eyes widened and quivered. He opened his creased mouth, like he was receiving the Holy Spirit or beginning to speak in tongues. Then a smile spread across his face. "Thank you. For showing yourself."

He gave me three hundred dollars and sent me on my way with a kiss to my hand because I refused to kiss him on the mouth. His thin, caterpillar-like lips searching for my affection made me squirm. I accepted the money because I needed it. He even let me take all the fancy soaps and shampoos from his room. I felt ashamed for about an hour, until I noticed I had enough in my account to pay for all my basics. No begging, no depending on anyone except a lonely man whose skin smelled like fabric softener and a hint of cigar smoke.

Not all of them smelled like that or had an egg for a cock. Some were rough and smelled like Fritos washed down with Jack and coke. The only times I felt shame were when my body inadvertently responded to the sex. Sometimes the body will take what it wants. The heartbeat quickens, a sheen of sweat as thin and tight as a wet, white swimsuit breaks out across my flesh and then euphoria rumbling from my clit like a sandstorm releasing chemicals into my brain that makes me forget everything.

After, as I shrank and wilted, I felt there was some rotten part of me that enjoyed it. Those eyes of the nuns and my peers were validated in their monstrous belief in my nature, a whore or worthless jackal like her mother. The ugliness was written on my face. I knew I didn't enjoy what I was doing in my mind, but my body did. My anger would set in when I would see that smug look on my client's face like they just did something. Like they just proved I was a slut. Nah, bro, you didn't do anything. You were just a john that made me nut and now I can pay my phone bill.

Eventually I left Tucson. I would miss Steve, my first everything. There were too many sounds and sights to navigate. I was no Alice and this was no Wonderland. You can't see the stars beyond the glare of the city lights. With a single bag, no plan or ambition, I was ready to hitchhike. I know. I *know*! Hitchhiking is a bad idea, not safe for a woman, but you don't understand. I can take care of myself. From the bottom of my lip all the way to the soft spot beneath my breasts, there is a thick, red rough scar that's not a scar. It's the fault line that opens a fate I still don't understand. It's my flesh zipper.

★   ★   ★

For some reason it only took one ride from a single truck driver I approached at a truck stop at the edge of Tucson. Looking back, I gravitated to old men because they felt safe. I was raised by women and never had a father, brothers or a grandfather. This particular driver looked almost as old as the one who tipped me well at the hotel. He had bags under his eyes that sagged into his aging cheeks. His weary demeanor made me think he should be retired by now. Like me, he probably needed the money. I approached him, not knowing what he would want from me in return.

"Excuse me, but I need a lift."

He looked me up and down and quickly looked away. "Oh, that's a young man's treat. Sorry darlin', but I'm not into that. If you need a meal, I can get you something from inside."

"No. I just need a ride. Where are you going?"

He sighed and looked at me again. "I got a granddaughter and if she needed a lift somewhere I would hope she would get it. And from someone who didn't have ill will. Also, I'm not looking for trouble. I don't carry hardly any cash with me."

I nodded, feeling relieved. "Not looking for trouble. Just finding my way."

He shrugged and opened the cab door, tossing a bag of snacks inside. "Where you want to go?"

Good question. A question everyone asks themselves at one time or another. Some give up because getting there seems impossible. Others drive hard, knowing there is enough fuel in the gas tank to get them there. And then there are those like me who just get swirly-eyed and have no clue. It's like looking out over a desert and mountains without a single sign of life. Where do you go when you don't know what is even out there?

"I don't know. Where are you heading?"

"Across the country, but the next big stop will be in Texas. That's how a guy like me treats himself. Best Mexican food and barbeque you have ever tasted. Out of this world."

"I guess I'll know when we get there." I walked to the other side of the cab and lifted myself in.

We sat side by side in silence as we left Tucson. George Strait played. Occasionally the truck driver hummed, keeping his eyes on the road. I slept when he drove and read a book when he slept. Turns out he continued to drive to pay for the grandchildren he and his wife were raising. He wanted to leave them with something since their parents left them with nothing.

After nearly a day of driving, we pulled off to a truck stop that looked like others, but it didn't feel that way. Large trees curled around it like a cocoon. I opened the window. I could smell the smokers roasting meat. I wanted to taste.

"C'mon. Let's park up and eat." His eyes shone as he said this; the rigor of youth straightened his back.

I left my suitcase in the truck, sure we would return. As I walked towards the restaurant, weakness gripped me. I touched my chin and neck, feeling that old itch. My stomach grumbled from hunger. Inside the restaurant was not remarkable, not as much as the smell. Nearly every seat on the long counter was filled; most of the booths too. A woman as short as me with the curves of one who has had a few children stood behind the counter pouring coffee and chatting to the customers. As soon as I walked in, she looked in my direction. Self-consciousness further weakened my muscles. Like everyone before, she stared at the curious mark on my face. Her smile melted like butter on hot pancakes, eyes dripping with questions or pity. I didn't know yet.

She rushed from behind the counter to greet us. "Welcome. There's a booth if you like?"

Now she tried hard not to stare rudely, giving us each menus. "I'll send someone over with ice water."

I scanned the menu. It all sounded delicious and I wanted to try everything. How do you choose just one? It overwhelmed me, making this simple choice, like trying to live a normal life in Tucson.

"Why don't you order for us? You know this place."

Doug seemed pleased to oblige my request.

After we ate, I paid. "Thank you for the ride. I'll just get my suitcase."

"You want to stay here? You sure? I don't think they'll let you stay. I never seen girls around here. Think the son doesn't allow it. And it's not safe. You seem like a good kid." There was genuine concern in his eyes.

"I'll be all right. You take care. Maybe I'll see you around again."

I walked back into the restaurant with suitcase in hand. There was a single seat next to a pecan pie in a glass cake stand. The woman looked at me, then my suitcase. Slowly I took the single seat.

"No plans just yet?"

"Just a slice of pie and coffee."

"Sure thing. My name is Donna, Donna Alcazar. Me and my boys run this place."

Donna brought me a thick slice of pecan pie and a coffee. "Coffee is on me."

"Thank you."

I sat there for hours with my paperback, savoring the dessert. Before I realized, the sun began to set, the brightness blinding me as it reflected off the stainless-steel wall in the kitchen.

Donna returned to refresh my ice water. "You don't have a place to go, do you? You have any family?"

I shook my head.

"Well, young women need to find their place in the world. There's a motel not far from here that rents rooms for the week. I'll make a phone call and see if I can get one for you. Is that all right?"

"That would be great. Thank you."

She flashed me a warm look and went to the cash register to make a call. That was the beginning of finding my place in the world.

3

Truckers make the detour because, unlike at the other stops, the food at the diner is exceptional. It was even featured on one of those food shows about the best places to eat on the road. They called it the most authentic Mexican food north of the border, with BBQ smoked to perfection. The recipes are from generations of one family led by Donna Alcazar. Leo, the eldest of three children, grows all the chilis in his greenhouse along with a horde of chickens and a few goats. In the woods adjoining the truck stop, a clearing has been made where they smoke some of the meat the old way, buried in a hole covered with hay, slowly burning. The flesh is infused with the earth until it flakes off the bone and melts in your mouth. The sauce is a rich syrup of spices, chili and sweetness made by Donna. Donna learned all about spices from the generations of women in her family until no one could remember who was the first to write them down. She once whispered it was the tamarind and habanero that gives it a distinctive tangy heat. Donna and her sons practically own the place since the owner, an aging widower without children, living out what time he has left in Galveston, is content to just collect his checks from the accountant. He takes his cut and leaves the rest for the family. Leo hopes the owner will sell or bequeath the restaurant, which pulls in almost as much as the gas station since Leo brokered a deal with a small manufacturer to package the sauce. Even though Donna was the first to work at the diner, Leo and her two other boys are the face of the business because they were all born in the States. Although she has been in Texas since she was a child, never knowing any other place, there is a worry she might be detained or deported. She keeps a low profile, like me. We dwell in the shadows. Sometimes shadows can be dangerous places because no one knows you are there, and if you don't exist, you're vulnerable.

The truck stop is a carcass that has fallen to the ocean floor and we are the life that thrives on the dissolving flesh. The bones have become coral that we call home. There is shelter, food, companionship and money. We look out for each other. I like the truck stop because it is familiar, small, like the place I spent the first part of my life. Tucson was far too big; it was an unmanageable world. Steve and I could never be anything more than lovers.

When it's been slow, Donna gives me plastic containers with leftovers she can't sell to take home.

One night, before I hit the asphalt and streetlights, she took the time to say, "Mija, be careful. You will always have work and a home with me if you want it. You can trust me."

Her warmth filled me like her food.

4

The post-holidays slowness had settled in. The trees' bony fingers, reaching for the heavens in consternation, took the shape of fleshless hearts with all the veins and capillaries on show. Every year begins stripped clean until buds erupt again as the heat returns. This time of the year people make their promises to themselves and others, forgetting their motivators are just in hibernation. They will awaken again, hungry or angry, wanting what they want. Just as the body wants what it wants.

I spent this time sitting in the last booth, drinking coffee with my thrift-store paperbacks. That is when I noticed a woman sitting at the bar looking forlornly at her plate then glancing at me enough to get my attention, but not long enough for others to notice. She didn't want others to notice. I had been with women before, but not as clients. Money sat next to her plate, which was empty, so I knew she was finished with her meal. When she looked over again, I slid from the bench and cocked my head to the side to signal she should follow me out.

She walked quickly past me and I followed her to a red Camry. The inside of her car was clean and smelled like a perfume I couldn't place but it wasn't cheap, maybe a gift from someone. I liked that. A small Puerto Rican flag hung from her rearview mirror. I sat in the passenger's seat while she sat behind the steering wheel, not wanting to look at me. I had felt that kind of shame before; it's unnecessary and stupid. Maybe I could fuck the shame out of her, or at least my sister could. I forgot to mention this truck stop is also known for something else: me.

I opened my coat and hoodie, then unhooked the front of my pink mesh bra trimmed with lace. A crack and a pop of my sternum allowed the little thing to come through. I finally had the attention of the woman. Her eyes slowly moved from the horn on the steering wheel to my chest, but she was not afraid. My sister mewed, knowing it was time to perform. She stretched her scrawny neck and wiggled her tongue the size of my thumb. She has weepy black beads for eyes, no lashes or eyebrows. She is surrounded by flaps of a translucent, waxy membrane with her in the center, like a little cabbage. I never had a Cabbage Patch doll or Garbage Pail Kids, but I did have her, a real one that was a little mix of both. *Little Shop of Horrors* is when I first got the idea my mother must have fucked an alien.

My internal organs are covered with the same membrane that breathes in sync with my lungs. Blue and red capillaries can be seen as they spread across my open chest, pulsating with my heartbeat. My breasts flop to the side to make way for the opening. I don't know how else we are connected because it is only her face I see. She doesn't speak. I only know what she may want or like or dislike by her movements. I can't control whether she makes an appearance or not.

The woman shifted her eyes to mine. "Sorry, it's not for me. My son. Will you come with me, please? I beg you." She placed a hand on my knee. Part of me was scared. I never go anywhere with any of them. A majority are harmless and are only lonely or horny, but there could be those who want more than sex. They want screams.

I trusted something in her; it was the way she looked at my sister with a sparkle in her eye, not fear. They're usually dreadfully afraid the first time. Dare I say I saw relief in her eyes upon the sight of my open chest cavity? Had she seen another one?

I could never predict who my sister would like. She moved her head up and down, rubbing her cheek against the flap of open flesh. She thought it was a good idea.

"I'll come with you, but I need to tell Donna the address. If you don't agree, I'm out."

Without a second of hesitation she nodded. "Of course, absolutely. I want you to feel safe." She acquiesced to my demands and we drove away from the truck stop.

★ ★ ★

Rebecca Flores continued to glance back at the woman she couldn't believe existed. Her boy wasn't an accident and she wasn't a freak or sinner for giving birth to him. The doctors first thought he had scoliosis, or a bone disease. Rebecca stopped seeing those doctors once it became clear he wasn't like anyone on Earth. This couldn't be described as a disease; he was a miracle. Descended from angels, she told herself. It was a miracle after all that she overheard a group of three truckers talking at a stop in Oklahoma.

"I don't know what she is, but I'm mesmerized. I guess she makes me feel like we ain't alone here. Something had to make her like that. And boy, does she know how to make a man feel good. Every time I pass through Texas, I get a good meal and her. Best damn barbeque."

"Jesus. You think she would do me?"

"Jack, you can't afford her. And if you want the special, it's extra. I was scared the first time. The little thing wiggles out like a worm from an apple. Man, it's strange and beautiful at the same time. She only takes referrals now and I'm not going to tell her about the likes of you. Don't want to be getting the clap."

Two of the men laughed at the one called Jack. "Greedy bastard," he mumbled.

Rebecca needed to find this stop. She forgot what she even came in for. She would wait outside to catch the trucker before he left. Strange and beautiful, like her son. When the three men exited the convenience store, she touched the arm of the bearded one.

"Excuse me, but couldn't help overhearing you talk about a truck stop in Texas. Best barbeque, I think you said."

"Oh yeah. You can't miss it. You'll be on 35 headed to San Antonio...."

Rebecca wasted no time finding this stop and looking for the woman who might have answers for her and her son. If not answers then companionship for her very special boy. Well, no longer a boy, but a man. And people need companionship; likeness. Gabriel stopped talking to her when he turned twenty.

When he moved back in, she hoped they would be best friends again, like when he was younger. Rebecca wanted grandkids, a normal family like the other families on her block. She worked hard like her parents to fit in, be a model American dream.

The woman at the truck stop was small and Latina. Despite what she did for a living, she seemed nice, bright. Rebecca wanted to ask her questions but thought it better she saw Gabriel first. Why should she trust her? Another reason she liked Gabriel living at home was because she knew he was safe. Who knew what could happen to him if the wrong type of people found out about him? It only happened once before. It left them both devastated. All a kid wants is to belong. After. After these two special people met would she ask her questions. Not probing, but Rebecca had to know.

★   ★   ★

After a twenty-minute drive with me fighting not to fall asleep to the Carpenters, we arrived at a small yellow house with a manicured yard. The sun wouldn't be up for another two hours and I was sleepy. I wanted to put on my flannel pajamas and brush my teeth. *This better be quick*, I groaned in my head.

The orderliness of the inside of the house resembled her car and yard. The living-room furniture was a matching three-seater brown sofa and recliner with a few picture frames that had photos of her and a small boy. This opened to a kitchen dining area with a table that only sat two. The dish caddy by the sink had plates and glasses for two. The boy in the photos, most probably now a man, might be the one I would be seeing.

She placed her jacket over a chair. In this light I could see a deep crevasse between her eyes and crow's feet that she seemed too young for. There was a lot of worry in this woman's life.

"Thank you for coming with me. Please don't be frightened. My son. You're for him, as I said before. He looks different, like you." Her brow furrowed the entire time she talked with what I assumed was the concern and sincerity a mother has for a child. I wouldn't know this myself, but I saw it in Donna's face when she spoke to her sons.

She pointed to a room just down the hallway. I hung my leather jacket on the other dining chair then walked to the hallway. I could hear her in the kitchen opening the freezer, ice clinking in a glass, then pouring herself something to drink. I knocked first.

"Come in."

It was the deep tenor of a man's voice. I held the handle for a moment, thinking about what she said – that he was like me. The heaviness of my eyes in the car vanished. I could feel my heart beat faster and the flutter between my breasts where my sister waited. She banged to get out, twisting in her membrane, pulling at the veins that connected us. I didn't know why she was so worked up. This had never happened before.

There he was. He wore loose jogging pants and no shirt. I didn't know what I expected, but he looked normal. He was easily twice my size and muscular. He made me think of some of those old porno covers. His belly had a softness to it, yet there was a defined gutter between his pecs. Large arms held the shape of the muscles beneath his skin. It was when he turned to shut his laptop that I saw why I was there. His wide back, which tapered to a V, was stripped of flesh with the exposed bones latticed like a chain-link fence. Between the gaps, muscle twitched below a membrane like mine. Thick, curly hair that would have fallen to his shoulders was tied in a ponytail, which allowed me to see two little brown eyes blinking at me and two holes which I imagined were nostrils at the base of his skull. Down his spine, in a vertical line, protruded teeth. It was a whole set of white with canines, molars and bicuspids that made me want to run my fingers against them like the keys of a piano or xylophone. What sound would he make if I touched him like this? Upon this sight my chest cracked open without warning. Her movements were so forceful I took a step back to steady myself. My sister wanted to see too. He turned around, bumping into his desk upon the sight of us.

"She said she found someone like me. Didn't think she had or would go through with inviting them here. What are your names?"

No one had ever asked me her name and I never named her. I just thought of her as an extension of me and not an autonomous being. We never spoke a word.

"I'm Sonora. She has no name. Just sister." I felt ashamed as I said this, selfish. She was the closest thing I had to family.

"I'm Gabriel and he's Gabe. Not unique but it felt right to call him something."

We stared at each other as if we were the only two in the world. For years I believed I was alone, an abomination pushed out by a jackal, but here he was. His mother wasn't a jackal; she was rather nice, a loving mother.

Fucking to come, fucking for money and fucking for connection all live in their own little houses. On occasion they meet. I wanted to connect and come with Gabriel.

I removed my unzipped hoodie. His eyes left my face to my exposed floppy breasts and my sister. I could see the excitement rising from between his legs. I wondered what surprise he had for me. I walked towards him and tugged at the drawstring on his pants as I unbuttoned my denim skirt and let it slide to my ankles.

"You don't have to if you don't want to. I don't know what she's paying. I would be happy to just talk."

Sister stretched her neck so far out, the membrane that connected felt uncomfortable under the strain. We both wanted closer. Her little head grazed the spot on his chest with dark curly hair. I looked towards the neatly made bed I hoped we would mess up, cover with our sweat.

"Show me," I said.

He fell to his knees and placed his forehead against my lower belly, both hands gripping my ass. I placed one foot on the bed. Without any prompting he looked up to me. I felt like a priestess offering my body. He took my clit between his full lips like a hamster at a water drip. His gentle sucking made me moan. He took the tip of his tongue and ran it the length of my labia, teasing me. Sister erratically rotated her head. I wish I knew what she felt and thought. With one hand I raised his wet chin to look at me again. I wanted his substantial weight on me, his brown skin and wild hair to cover me like a flesh quilt of Mexican and Puerto Rican brown. His thick lips, as full as mine, wasted no time finding my mouth and breasts as we fell onto the bed.

I wrapped my legs around him, cradled him with my thighs, bucking my hips as hard as I could because this close just wasn't good enough. Sister mouthed his chest. Shortened breaths escaped her lips. His tongue now found sister. Small kisses to her face. My fingers hooked within the bones of his back, giving me more leverage to take him to the hilt, release all my wetness that I could drown in for all I cared. As I held onto his back, I could feel dampness on my fingertips. Was I harming him? He wasn't crying out in pain, only moaning with pleasure as he sucked on my neck. I brought my hands to my lips; it was salty and viscous. Gabe was crying, but his tears tasted of semen. I touched his back again, brushing against the teeth with my fingertips. This made Gabriel cry out and convulse, as he stared into my eyes. His entire body trembled in flesh waves. I knew he was coming because the warmth spilled down my legs.

I pushed on his chest so he would know it was my turn. Without concern if Gabe could breathe in this position, I straddled Gabriel and leaned closer so he could tease my nipples. His fingertips explored the ridges of my open chest. He was still filling me, stiff as ever. I used one hand to bring myself to orgasm, something I'm *very* good at. It started so small and tight, a little scream growing inside of me that had the voice of a woman who sounded like me but wasn't me. Unzipped from the base of my clit to the base of my neck, a shockwave of pleasure pummeled me to silence. I couldn't scream even though something was shouting inside. My feet spasmed to the point they hurt. I pressed harder, letting his cock continue to unzip me until I fell into his chest. I remembered Gabe.

"Sorry," I panted.

I rolled to his side. Sister was furling her floppy head back inside and my chest was closing. Gabriel faced me and touched the part of my zipper that doesn't open from my bottom lip to the jugular notch. Usually I'm dressed and collecting money by this time. Today, I just wanted to lie there and fall asleep.

I wanted to know more about Gabriel and Gabe. "Does he speak to you?"

"Not in words. Just a feeling, like instinct. I hear my own voice sometimes, but I don't know if it's him or just myself."

"Was this your first time? Because you seemed to know what you were doing."

He groaned and rolled his eyes. "God, what has my mother been saying? No, not my first, but my first with anyone like me. Not a single lover has seen me naked like this. Feels good. And you? How do you work with this, given your profession?"

"It's part of it. Sometimes. I have truckers that come and ask for the special. That means her, if she's willing. I also have regulars. Sometimes we don't even fuck. They just look and pleasure themselves. I don't ask or judge."

He inched closer to me. "When did she first appear?"

I moved closer and kissed him, our mouths opening to each other, our bodies aching to fit again. "I better go. I need to sleep."

He tried to say something, but I stopped him with another kiss. Fuck, he was a great kisser and I hadn't been kissed since Steve. The closest I ever came to love was listening to 'Son of the Morning Star' with Steve in our little video store world.

"Maybe I'll see you again."

I scanned the room as I rose to dress. Against the wall there was a desk with multiple screens attached to a bunch of computer equipment that took up most of the space. His bed was just large enough for two. A pull-up bar was attached to the doorframe and a weight rack stood against the wall with a simple bench press. The single window was flanked by bookcases filled with books. It looked like he had his own little world in here with no reason to leave. I felt a pinch of envy.

I walked to the door, leaving him sitting up in bed.

"You sure you have to leave?" he called to me.

Damn, I wasn't sure. I had a million questions. Why hadn't I answered his? Had I been closed off for so long? Before walking out, I turned. "Yes, I have to leave. And she first appeared when I was five." I shut the door, trying not to second-guess my decision.

Within seconds the shower in the bathroom attached to his room was running. Good. He got the message.

Rebecca sat at the dining-room table watching the sunrise with coffee in hand, an empty highball glass in front of her. She had been crying.

I coughed softly to alert her of my presence. "Well, I guess I'll be off?"

She turned to me, that pleading, furrowed expression returning to her face. "Thank you. Thank you for spending time with my boy. I hate him being so isolated." Her voice cracked with released sobs.

I was still sweaty and wet from sex. Should I go to her to comfort her with her son's essence still clinging to my body? I sat close but not too close. "Thank you for finding me."

Her face lit up when I said this. "Can I make you some breakfast? Coffee? I got a fresh pot." The look in her eyes was desperate, like she wanted to talk. I got the feeling they kept to themselves; others might reveal Gabriel's secret. But I wanted to talk too. I had to know. Did she fuck a demon or get abducted by aliens? Besides, I was hungry, and she didn't distract me the way Gabriel and Gabe did. Breakfast and coffee would be nice. She made me over-easy eggs, bacon and toast. Of course, since she was a good mother, there was grape jelly. It all smelled wonderful. I wondered what I did in life to have nice women willing to feed me. She didn't eat, just filled up her mug and sat next to me.

"I pulled him outta school when a bunch of boys ripped off his shirt in front of the whole class in sixth grade. He was so scared and hurt. We made a deal with the school and when it came to high school he went back in another county. Teasing still followed because he refused to shower or participate. Eventually he dropped out, got his GED. He finished college a few years ago and now does website maintenance stuff from his room. Smart boy; a good boy. He needs someone to bring him out of his shell."

"I started driving when he was old enough to be left alone at home. I knew I had to make something of my boy. No way did I want to lose him, and I knew in my heart I would lose him if he didn't have a passion or job to keep him busy."

It was my turn to ask a question. "Do you know who his father is?"

"Do I? Hell yes, I know. His dad was my school principal. I know what you're thinking: pedophile, but it didn't happen that way. I was working at a bookstore after graduation when he recognized me. He started coming in regularly with his kids and, well, I got pregnant. He tried to live two lives between me and his wife, but it was no good. He always wanted a son, but not like this. My auntie said Gabriel was born different because of our sin. My mother told her to go to hell and get fucked by the devil. She might like it. Gabriel's only male role model was my dad, a truck driver. How about you?"

I wanted to cry, feeling sorry for myself. I thought I had found a missing part of my past, but I was really an orphaned daughter of a jackal.

"I was found in the desert in my dead mother's arms as she tried to cross the border. I was raised in a girls' home. Left at eighteen."

She poured me another cup of coffee, then turned to her purse. I could tell she didn't know what to say to this.

"So you know nothing about your body?"

"I was hoping you would have answers for *me*. Sorry."

There was no mistaking the disappointment in her eyes. "Tell me what I owe you, plus I want to give you a little more. I was wondering if maybe I could have a way to contact you. For other times for him. And please, if you need anything, don't hesitate to call on me. My son is a quiet one and suspicious of people after all he's been through. Don't take no offense to his shyness."

Gabriel was anything but shy. I was thinking of the way we wrestled, with moans and curses, trying to test the boundaries of our skin, like maybe we could melt into each other, find out what's inside, how our odd parts connected. And those hands with their solid grip on my flesh. Those teeth jutting from his spine and how they felt against my palm.

Money slid before me. I stopped reliving that sexual experience I would never forget.

I slid the money back. "Can I ask how you heard about me?"

"Yeah. A truck stop in Oklahoma. Heard some boys talking like they were hanging out in a locker room."

This didn't surprise me. Word of mouth was how I generated most of my business. Repeat business was the way I made the bulk of my money. Rarely did I have to stand outside for hours any longer. I gave her my number before I called a taxi to drive me to my motel room to sleep most of the day until I headed back to the truck stop.

I dreamed of my mother, of me sucking on her breast in the shade. A hot breeze mingled with dust blows hair across her face. Her head is thrown back because she's thirsty, and my sucking is painful as I take the last of her nourishment. There's no hope and she doesn't want to die until we have crossed that border. She is mumbling in Spanish. It is a prayer to anything or anyone that will hear to get me to safety.

I woke up while it was still dark. The streetlight crept across my ceiling through my blinds, casting claw-like shadows. Something sliced through.

My memory of the first time anyone saw my sister.

★   ★   ★

I had finished watching porn. It gets pretty monotonous after a while. I chose Steve, the owner of the video store and part-time journalist, to take my virginity. Hence why he had all those magazines, besides his love for music. He offered to hold a copy of the new horror releases for me when I came in. His presence was comforting, and I felt myself drawn to it, wanting to know more about the stack of magazines, the store, his body. I wanted to move on from porn to the real thing. The chemistry between us was like a song that makes you stop whatever you are doing and listen. It was the song you play over and over because it makes you feel good and you can't seem to get enough of it. It speaks to you. And songs do not reject you or judge. It was time to take him into the dark confessional and push back the screen. Confess.

It would be the last time I ventured into the little room, or so I thought. Steve knew me better by this time, letting me look alone after closing to avoid being harassed by the men who came in. We made small talk over the counter, enough to know we liked each other. He gave me my privacy, always a gentleman. He gave me space in the back room and now I felt comfortable enough to let him in. To see me. Steve locked the front door and turned the sign on the door to *Closed*.

"Steve, do you mind helping me back here?"

He gave me a smile like he usually did when I paid for my films. "No problem."

The music of sex hummed from the TV. Lights just above the illumination of a Christmas tree lit the room. I asked him plainly, "Show me?"

He looked confused. "Show you...the new ones?"

I unbuttoned the top button of my Wrangler jeans. Shock crossed his face. He ran his hands through his black scruffy hair. I couldn't blame the guy for not knowing how to react. I assumed it would be a no.

"I didn't think you thought of me that way. This is a surprise... wow." He looked good in the shadow of the dark light, a boyish face with a thick goatee. I wanted to feel it brushing against my neck and thighs, like I had thought about many times before. I wanted to wipe away the wetness from my pussy from his mouth then kiss him. I ached for him in that moment.

"Is that a yes or no?" I hoped he would say yes. I needed it to be a yes. I had been practicing the art of multiple orgasms in my efficiency apartment for far too long.

He stepped closer, placing his hand around my waist. "I'll show you whatever you want. I've played this out in my mind before. I've never asked you out because I didn't want to be a creep."

My first kiss. My first sexual encounter. The first time sister made her desire to be seen known to a man. I pressed my lips against his and wrapped my hands around the back of his neck. He kissed my bottom lip and continued to inch kisses and flick his tongue down the fine line on my chin and neck. I unzipped my ribbed sweater. With an eager mouth he used his lips to stimulate the red scar, then moved to my nipples as he cupped my breasts. I closed my eyes, allowing the sensation of flesh on mine to take over, our mutual attraction to have its way. He dropped to his knees, unzipped my jeans and pulled them down.

We fucked sitting upright with my thighs thrown over his as we stabilized our grinding pelvises with our arms at our sides. He felt even better than I imagined. From a distance we probably resembled a flesh spider. He looked at my scar, the redness as it swelled, pulsated like a throbbing worm. His eyebrows knitted and he stopped. I continued to move, enjoying his body. He sat upright and squeezed my knees as the crack of my sternum rose above the static of the dead video. The membrane glistened, like my lubricated lips that eagerly swallowed Steve's cock.

She was tiny, her head no larger than a golf ball. He pulled his body away but not his gaze. I stayed there, legs akimbo feeling an overwhelming sadness. "I know I'm ugly. Just say it and get it over with."

He shook his head, eyes wild. "This isn't real. What are you? Who are you? What the fuck is that!"

"I don't know who she is." I closed my legs and got to my knees to leave.

"Wait. Can I have a closer look?"

No one had ever laid eyes on her. She was my little friend who had always been there. The first time I saw her was when I was five and didn't know what was happening. Being so young, I didn't feel fear. I thought I was like the picture of Jesus with the burning heart protruding from his chest.

"You can look, but no touching."

Steve crawled towards me, his cock swinging between his thighs. He came face to face with her, studying with an open mouth my strange anatomy. Little sister pushed her neck forward and rolled her head in his direction.

"I think it's okay if you have one little touch."

He looked at me, then her, licking his lips. With his index finger he stroked the top of her head. I shuddered and placed my hand between my legs. I wanted to continue with our sex even though I wasn't sure he wanted to. Discreetly I touched myself as he ran a fingertip in a swirl around her head. He placed a palm against the membrane that encased my internal organs.

That was when he noticed my hand moving faster, deeper into my pussy. Steve placed his hand over mine while kissing my neck tenderly. He was erect again. He slid opposite me, while we both masturbated to the sight of each other.

5

The voice was a male. My heart thumped because I knew it was Gabriel.

"Hello, Sonora?"

"Hi." I didn't want to seem excited, even though I was. My belly and chest fluttered.

"I was hoping you would come over tonight. I can pick you up at the truck stop about eight. My mother isn't here. If that's okay."

It was perfectly okay. I looked forward to a night of good sex. I didn't feel like working with my mind and body adjusting to the knowledge I was not alone. I had Donna fix us two brisket and corn on the cob platters to go.

She raised her eyebrows with a smile as she packed the food in takeaway boxes in a plastic bag. "Who is he, or she?"

I took a twenty out of my coat pocket. "Just a friend."

"Have fun and be safe." She pushed the cash away. "You know I don't take your money. I feed my family." I knew she wouldn't take the twenty. I'd be sure to buy her something nice the next time I made it into town. "Oh. If I can give you one piece of advice. Don't be afraid. Open yourself."

Gabriel waited in the parking lot in the Camry. We drove the same route as his mother the previous night. "Thanks for meeting me. I'll be honest, I haven't been able to sleep. I've never met someone like me."

"I feel the same. At least you have family."

When I entered Gabriel's room there was a mirror above his bed and another where the headboard used to be. "You've been busy."

"I think Gabe would enjoy it more. Anyway, I don't know how much?" He offered a stack of fifties. God, how those brown eyes and body pulled me by the clit again. Tiny wires between my legs and nipples sparked at once.

"I don't want your money. Turn around." He took his glasses off before doing as I asked. I undressed myself.

His back faced me with his hair tied in a knot. Gabe locked eyes with me, then moved to my breasts that wobbled as my chest opened with a moist crack. Sister mewed like a cat, pulling hard against the membrane. She wanted closer. I placed one hand on Gabriel's hip and the other down his loose tracksuit shorts. I stroked his cock slowly with my head leaning against his ribs. Sister rubbed her face, which has the softness of foreskin, against Gabe. One of his teeth scraped sister's bare scalp. Gabriel continued to moan with both of his hands clutching the edge of his desk, my hand wet from stimulating him. Gabe closed his eyes. The teeth twitched along Gabriel's back when sister licked the teeth, scraping her little head across them again, relishing the closeness she never felt with another of our kind. An orgy of freaks who were finding comfort in one another. Gabriel turned around to lead me to the bed.

I hooked my fingers into the exposed latticed bone on his back again as we rocked each other to orgasm, twisting and turning, our bodies a Rubik's Cube of parts. A fluttering beneath my sternum alerted me to my sister longing to breathe and see. I often wondered how much of this she felt. Were our nervous systems connected? How much of the chemicals of sex washed over her like they did me? I pushed his chest away from my body to let her loose. He continued his grinding, not wanting to stray from the drumbeat of our wet fucking, or my eyes. Little sister let out a cry as she emerged like a turtle from her shell, my body.

After, part of me wanted to stay, but I felt compelled to go. The sooner I dressed the sooner I could get out the door without too much conversation. I grabbed my acid-wash denim skirt when Gabriel stopped me from leaving.

"Can I show you something on the computer?"

"Sure," I said as I continued to dress.

"Don't be alarmed. Tell me to stop it and I will." Before showing me whatever he wanted to show me, he muted the sound.

I watched the largest of the three screens that sat in the center. I moved closer to get a better look to ensure I was really seeing what my eyes told my brain was in front of me. A man and a woman like us with misshapen other beings attached to them clung to each other, bound and looking like they had been dragged through hell. They appeared bruised, bloodied and, by the look in their eyes, drugged.

"Turn it off. Turn it off!" I screamed. My entire being shook with rage and confusion. "Why did you show me that? What the hell is that? Mutant snuff? You sick fuck. To think I was beginning to like you. You get off to that? Is that what you think about when we're fucking?" My chest pounded, as did my head.

He fumbled with the mouse, trying to stop the video. There was no sound thankfully and no wonder he muted it. I turned away, trembling, feeling on the verge of blacking out. I had only felt like this a few times before. The doctors put it down to my weak heart. Once was when I had a gun pulled on me and the other when a dude got rough, not wanting to pay. The fear for my life sparked my adrenal glands to pump wildly before the world turned black. On both occasions at the truck stop my chest burst open violently, catching the men off guard. I could only look forward with splintered vision that wouldn't move, but in my periphery sister's little head swayed back and forth, leaving the men stunned, their eyes blank and bodies rigid. I blinked enough out of my daydream-like state to run from their vehicles. Neither ever returned.

Gabriel was behind me, his hands on my forearms. "No, No! I'm worried about you. This isn't the only one! There are more. I sent an anonymous tip to the FBI and local police. Nothing. I wanted to know if you'd heard anything or have seen anything strange. I've been searching my whole life for others. To find them...like this." His voice cracked like he was about to cry.

My anger died down. I turned to face him. He had the same expression on his face that his mother did the night I met her. I could tell he didn't like this any more than I did.

"I can't let this go. People like us are being targeted for some weird shit and it's getting circulated over the Dark Net."

The horror of the video fled and now the knowledge I wasn't alone hit me like a semi. How was any of this possible? What were we? "You know anything else about us?"

He shook his head. "I've been searching for years. This is the closest I've come to seeing others like us. You?"

"Nope. You're the first. I thought it was just me, a by-product of something awful."

He grabbed both of my hands. "You both are anything but awful. And believe me when I say I thought the exact same thing. I don't tell my mother much because there's no way she could understand."

"It doesn't bother you, what I do?"

"Part of me doesn't like it, but another understands. It's your body and your life."

6

My client and I were walking to his truck when I saw her in the distance. Shit. The boring slacks, sensible shoes and a bob that could only mean a police officer. Her green bomber jacket cut at the waist was cute though. It had been a long time since I had been arrested for solicitation and I didn't want to fork out the cash for a lawyer. I was feeling this job less and less since meeting Gabriel. If I was with Gabriel, I wasn't working. Luckily, I had rolls of cash held tightly in rubber bands in my shoe collection. If I ever got robbed, no one was going to look there. Under my breath I told my client to walk in the other direction while I waited for the woman to approach. Real wisdom is knowing what battles to fight.

"Hello, officer, how can I help you tonight? The special is real good this evening, at the restaurant, of course."

"Sonora, correct?"

Fuck. How did she know my name?

"I'm Calgary Espinoza, FBI. I was wondering if we could speak in my car. I'm with someone you might know – Gabriel." She turned and pointed to her unmarked car. There were two people I couldn't identify sitting in there. This had to be about what Gabriel showed me on his computer. I thought no one cared.

"Lead the way, Calgary."

The car was filled with the aroma of that night's special from the restaurant. It made my mouth water because I hadn't eaten yet. A bellyful of food and fucking does not always go well. The driver of the vehicle was a youngish white guy chowing down like he was having sex for the first time.

"Calgary, this place lives up to its reputation," he said. "Best damn pork and brisket tacos. That green salsa. Damn."

"It's green because it's made from tomatillos. Donna and her sons grow them."

The guy looked at me like I was speaking another language.

I glanced at Gabriel, who had his hair down. He said, "You aren't in any trouble, Sonora. I promise."

Calgary turned to face us. "I have no interest in your work, but I do have an interest in your…uniqueness. That video, we've been following that operation for some time and even have an officer inside the group, but we need individuals like yourselves to work the other end."

Gabriel put his hand over mine. "It's so much worse than I thought. Please keep an open mind." Whatever was happening, Gabriel had already said yes.

"I'm listening." Which was tough to do with the officer in the passenger's seat making hot love to his food with all kinds of eating noises distracting us all.

Calgary stopped to look at her partner. "Jake, do you mind with the lip smacking for five minutes?"

"You're the boss, sorry." He closed the cardboard takeaway box and wiped his greasy mouth before switching to the coke.

"Gabriel already told us he showed you the videos. These skinheads are a bunch of wannabe *Breaking Bad* assholes experimenting with opioids, meth and fentanyl. Somehow, and we don't know because our undercover guy isn't that tight yet, this group found out about individuals like yourselves. They're using you as guinea pigs. They want an empire built on the back of perceived undesirables who no one really knows exists."

Gabriel squeezed my hand and I knew what was next.

"We want you two to get taken in by them. We have to get them on drug charges because you can't charge someone with a hate crime against individuals who don't officially exist. There is no definition of who you are."

"Sounds like you want to make us guinea pigs as well?"

"They won't stop, and they have money. It's bigger than some ignorant, inbred, neo-Nazi or KKK chapter meeting in someone's kitchen. You have Sunday school, Boy Scout-looking guys trying to sugarcoat what they are. Some fascist from a time long gone who was living in South America all this time left his grandson a bunch of cash. Ever heard of Spencer Richardson? He is the one we need. It's not the low levels we want; we want the man with the money and influence. He's organized, hasn't worn a combat boot in his life and I don't believe he has a single tattoo on his body. Alt-right fuck's trying to make hate mainstream by looking like an Eddie Bauer ad. Being a racist hate-spewing cunt isn't a crime, so we have to get him on something that will keep him and his gang behind bars long term. Let the Latin Kings have a pop at them. But first we need hard evidence of their narcotics operation to make sure they get locked up with no wiggle room for release any time soon."

Shit *was* bad. The climate was ICE and it wouldn't be long until the world decided to freeze over in fearmongering and hate. People were ridiculed for wanting to change, for loving who they wanted to love, for seeing what was inside and making it a reality on the outside. There was no tolerance for the other. People, children, thrown in cages and locked in hotels denied any help or legal assistance. Some of them died from the flu with no doctor called to help them. Fuck those bastards. I saw the rallies on TV, heard of the deaths, watched those kids with barely a handful of pubes on their balls marching like a line of SS with tiki torches in their hands. It wasn't just that our skin was a different color; we were different in a fundamental way. But I felt too small to make a difference; just one person. How could I change anything?

"I can get you a new identity. A new life away from the truck stop if you want." I could see Calgary's expression was of sincere concern with a little pity. Everyone pities the whore. I glanced at Gabriel, who looked like he hadn't taken a breath in all this time.

I never knew why the desert spared me. The sun is merciless, but like the sisters said all those years ago, I survived. "I'll do it. What's your plan?"

"This truck stop. Our agent will pick you up here with Gabriel acting as your pimp. Both of you will be taken to wherever they're packaging the drugs and keeping people against their will.

But this will be the first time our agent will see this place. Most likely the boss won't make an appearance. We believe everything we'll need to put the entire operation down is there, including incriminating information to lock up Spencer because he's too good at keeping his hands clean. The agent is going by the name of Brandon Walters. Expect a clean-cut khaki-wearing guy and not someone who looks outrageous. Three days."

★   ★   ★

Rebecca paced around the kitchen. "I don't like the sound of this. You kids just found each other and now some Fed wants to put you in danger?"

"Rebecca, we already are in danger. These Nazi fucks aren't going anywhere. They have money. We need to get charges to stick and take them out for a long time."

"Gabriel, you're all I have. Please. Let the authorities do this."

"Mom, they've tried, and these fucks keep getting away with it. No. It has to stop. I feel this is right."

I wanted to talk to the other woman in my life. The truck stop always had steady traffic, so there was no good or bad time to go. I knew Donna would give me the time I needed. Gabriel drove me back to the truck stop so I could speak to her. When I walked into the diner she was chatting to the customers at the counter as if they were family. I waved at her to get her attention.

"Donna, may I speak to you?"

"Sure, mija. Sounds serious. Why don't we go for a walk?"

We walked through the parking lot to the surrounding woods where Leo had his smoke pits. Something cooked slowly. It smelled delicious enough for me to crawl on my hands and knees and dig up, devour in one sitting, bones and all. The calm clearing was filled with smoke and cicadas. The sunshine was warm on my skin.

Donna had her back to me, staring at the pits.

I wasn't sure how to start. "Donna. I need advice."

She remained silent and in the same place for a moment before turning to face me. Her pupils grew, then transformed to spirals. Swirly eyes from my drawing all those years ago. From my childlike mind that held no fear or doubt in the world. Open to the world and all possibilities.

I felt myself shaking all over. "Donna?"

"Yes, my child?" she said as she unbuttoned her shirt.

"Your eyes." My chest ached the longer I stared. I felt light-headed, like my pupils wanted to split into rings.

"The windows to the soul. And we're the lucky ones with our souls pushing through into the world. They've hibernated long enough. Some are completely out in this world and others still attached to their flesh. Like us. So beautiful, don't you think?"

"Are we evil?"

Her face softened and she stepped closer to me. Close enough to touch my cheek. "No, not us. But as you experienced, the ones without a soul are. But don't be sad. Not all is lost. Souls are eternal. And your beautiful soul, as it unites with others in sex, plants the seeds in their human cells so the ones we touch may also experience this evolution. But only those it deems worthy."

"What are we?"

"Not from this universe. Not even close. Mine does not tell me the secrets, only to enjoy this flesh while it lasts. Is this what you wanted to discuss?"

I looked below her breasts to see her belly button was a large vagina. A penis instead of a tongue poked through and the labia moved like the lips of a mouth. A small croak escaped my mouth and I could feel my chest splitting open beneath my sweatshirt.

"No. Something worse. Something is coming for us. We're being hunted. Murdered for being different."

Her smile dimmed. "I knew this day would come sooner

or later. Like the meat slowly changing beneath the Earth, our kind also wait in the heat to break forth from the soil. Tell me everything. We can't waste any time."

I told Donna all about the recording Gabriel showed me and my past.

★　　★　　★

Seeing Donna made me rethink leaving Steve and the video store. If whatever I am is catching, he surely has it. After our first encounter, I met him every day after closing. We lay in the back room surrounded by porn covers and music. I liked the back of the video store. It was small and manageable, safe like a cocoon. On a blanket I would lie with my legs splayed, my feet on the floor. With his mouth and tongue trailing along my skin, he opened my flesh zipper from the bottom of my lip to just beneath my breastbone. The cracking of bone as I split open excited him instead of scaring him off. All my insides and what others considered ugly were exposed. He would smile before kissing me hard on the lips as his fingertips crawled along the exposed breathing membrane inside of my chest and the curves of my breasts. The other part of me, my sister, swayed side to side for him to reach out to her too. And he did. All of me he touched, stimulated. His eyes were so black as he entered me, a black cocoon in themselves, full of wasps, injecting me with desire. Their venom made me want him more and more. He didn't drink or do drugs – hell, the guy was a vegan – but he took all his unspent vice out on my body. I rode him until he lay intoxicated from pleasure, his body shaking from losing fluids. Sometimes I worried I was the one doing the injecting. His body spasmed as he screamed out during his orgasm. After, we lay and shared our love for all things. Turns out we both loved Danzig. The deep bluesy tone of Glenn's voice sounded like Steve's mouth on my body, the texture and pressure changing to fit the mood. He was what I didn't know I wanted. But who the hell ever knows what they really want until they make choices, taste different apples? Even then, everything organic is susceptible to rot.

I left him with a note inside the bag with the videos I needed to return. I was falling for him, but too afraid of what happens after you fall. Your body splats onto the cement hard. Everything shatters and it's never the same again. I hated and loved myself too much for that. I had also come to the conclusion that a ring on the finger is one of the many rings that leads to hell, if hell even existed. If the animals don't need fidelity, why do we? I promise the man who created the ring got the idea from shackles. Aren't they the same shape?

Now, if he didn't hate me too much, I needed to reach out to see if he had changed or if his cells withstood the mutation.

7

Brandon leaned against a taupe Lexus in a brown fleece and navy trousers. This was not the face of anarchy and hate that we imagine. I was expecting the stereotypical skinhead I could spot a mile away, but hate isn't always ugly and that was what scared the shit out of me. He could have been someone's teacher, a police officer, teaching Sunday school. I felt better about what I was doing.

"Hey. Thank you for being part of this operation. I can't wait to get this over with because these freaks that call themselves the alt-right are making me hate life, and humanity for that matter. My wife and kids are living their lives without me and I miss them like hell."

He unlocked the car. "Right," he said, "we're going to what they call an election quarters, but in reality it's a level of hell. A suburban *Texas Chainsaw Massacre*. And prepare yourselves for seeing…others like you in bad condition, in cages." He paused and looked at us. Up close I could see the bags beneath his eyes, the bloodshot whites. He looked older than the photo we were shown.

It would be an hour's drive. Gabriel held my hand in the backseat. The last thing I felt like doing was talking. I leaned back in the silence and closed my eyes. I never thought about these big world problems because my world was the truck stop, the staff my extended family. Sister was my only blood relative that I knew of. Before that my only world was the video store with Steve and school, with only acquaintances and the teachers. I opened my eyes when I could feel the vehicle significantly slow down. Had to be side roads or residential.

The home was huge. A mini McMansion with a black BMW parked in front. The development was one of those places where you chose every detail of your home, down to the shower heads before it was even built. All with respectable cars parked in drives.

Brandon parked in front of the house. He was still holding the steering wheel while he looked at the house like we were walking into Hitler's bunker. "All right. Here we are."

Gabriel gripped the headrest behind the passenger's seat. "What's the plan?"

"The only reason I've been allowed to know this location is because I told them I was bringing you. The plan is—"

The front door opened. A young man who looked like he worked at Abercrombie & Fitch walked out with another older man who looked like he was part of Hitler's hillbilly family tree.

"Fuck. What the hell are they doing? It was only supposed to be Dean, the stupid one. That kid is Richard's nephew. Dammit. I need to contact Calgary fast—"

Abercrombie boy approached the passenger window and the other the driver's side. Brandon put his phone down quickly. The ugly skinhead tapped on his window with a leering meth smile. His t-shirt hung loose around the collar.

"You having a conference out here? Why don't you bring in the guests of honor?"

This would not end well. I could feel it. We were stuck. Brandon wasn't wearing a wire either. We got out of the car and followed them inside. I looked around, wondering how soundproof these houses were. My chest thumped in erratic beats, and I couldn't tell if it was my heart or my sister warning me. Probably both.

The young kid locked the door behind us. When I looked back, the ugly one had pulled out a knife and cut cleanly through Brandon's throat without a moment of hesitation. As easy as buttering bread. I screamed, bringing my hand to my mouth. Instinctively Gabriel lunged. Abercrombie pulled out a Taser, sticking it into Gabriel's side. He convulsed and fell on the ground on top of the bleeding Brandon. I wanted to cry for Brandon's family as I watched the tear in his throat gush blood beneath Gabriel. I wanted to kill these grotesque people.

"Fucking snitch. And thank God that brown hulk is down. He was going to be trouble. You. Pretty little ugly thing, come with me."

They frogmarched me to the back of the house with next to no decoration. A door I assumed led to a basement was to our right. "Down."

The lights shined brighter than the upstairs. Before I stepped into the cavernous unfinished basement, I had to catch my breath. In six large cages were others like me. Steve was in the center of the cement floor. There were swatches of white bandages on his half-nude body. His black eyes, which I loved so much, were now multiplied, six of them ringing his neck like a tattoo. They appeared bloodshot and cloudy. I wanted to fuck up these Nazis so bad I could taste it. Why couldn't I be a jackal? Steve recognized me; all eight eyes followed my movements. I couldn't read the emotion behind the drugs.

The skinhead with glassy eyes stood next to a greasy blonde who was watching over the hostages. She walked over to me and spit in my face. With little control my chest cracked open. The blonde ripped my top to expose my chest. They watched my sister in wonder and contempt. I couldn't move or kick or bite, just stand there and be a victim with my hands held behind my back by Abercrombie. I never saw myself as one until now.

"You know why we hate you?" Abercrombie said to me in my ear. "Because you're disgusting and you're multiplying. Your gross existence is something that needs to be eradicated."

I could only look at Steve. His anger was rising to the surface of his body and his eyes, despite his helplessness to do anything.

"You know what, you Nazi piece of shit? It's gonna be you. We will rise and fuck all of you up. Just wait. You won't even see it coming. Beneath the ground. Our rage is a simmering stew of meat, rising with the heat of the very core of the Earth."

"Hold the thing, Darlene." The skinhead walked towards a table with dirty dishes and dried food gathering flies. He picked up a chef's knife and pointed it towards my chest. The sight of the blade quickened my breath. They'd better not dare. No fucking way.

"Gross, I don't want to touch it or her. I hate fucking dirty foreigners. Mexicans are the worst."

"I'm a citizen, you bitch! I have the same rights as you with a birth certificate to prove it, you Nazi cunt." I spat in her face as she did mine. With all the rancor building inside of me, I could feel myself begin to sway.

Her eyes, just as glassy as the ugly dude's, narrowed. The cheap mascara and shitty application left eyelash marks on her eyelids. Remnants of blue eyeshadow smudged at the sides. In two steps the woman stood directly in front of me with my sister in her grasp, pulling her thin neck as she mewed and cried as best she could without full vocal chords.

"Do it," the woman spat.

With one arc of his arm, the ugly dude lopped off my sister's head. Blood sprayed them both like an out-of-control water hose. They watched with wonder again as my body jerked and spasmed in pain. I screamed with a force that felt like the veins in my neck would burst and blood would fountain out of my mouth.

He took the woman into his arms and began to kiss her deeply as our blood bathed them both. In those seconds something inside of me broke. My body had been desecrated, Gabriel knocked out, Steve in a cage pumped full of drugs. I don't know what happened exactly but from what Steve told me later, I began to convulse, my eyes rolling into my head then splitting into concentric circles. My chest snapped shut like a clam. The couple stopped their make-out session to watch.

"Fuck! She dying?"

"Who cares? We'll throw her in the river."

The convulsing turned to bucking and the shrieking to a volume so loud Steve had to cover his ears, but it was a cry the couple could not hear. He looked around to see the others like us holding their ears in pain as well. When he looked back, I had ripped my hands free from Abercrombie and bashed his head against the wall with such force it popped upon impact, breaking an exposed pipe. Water spewed out uncontrollably. Without a second for them to react I had taken the knife from the skinhead and jabbed it into the chest of the woman, then whipped to the side, thrusting it into the ribs of the skinhead. As he doubled over, I lashed him across the face with the back of my hand.

He fell to the floor, hands over his face. "Stop! Stop! Get her some help!"

I remember standing over him, watching him cower and blubber with a mixture of blood and snot on his chin and lips. A large blood bubble grew from his nose. The floor beneath my feet was covered with the rising water. I took my left foot and placed it over his face, bursting the bubble.

"Give me the keys to the cages or I'll finish what I started."

He unhooked a set of keys at his waist, feebly handing them to me.

"Where's your phone, asshole?"

With trembling fingers he pointed to a backpack with neo-Nazi patches. He held on to the handle of the knife in his body.

I unlocked the cages and motioned for them all to get out. Steve stood on unsteady legs to face me, hurt in his eyes. Instead of walking away, he kissed me. Kissed me like he did in the video store. This time we were both covered in blood.

"I guess we're not so different after all," I said. I wanted to cry, run away. "I'm sorry I made you like this." I ran my hands across his chest and the eyes blinked with heavy lids.

"Stop. It was so fucking worth it. You're worth it. I never stopped hoping you would walk through the door again and lead me to the back room, our place in the world."

I grabbed his hand, knowing he was the only one for me. "I love you, Steve. Let's get out of here."

My thoughts returned to Gabriel as we walked towards the door. I had to get to him. I let go of Steve's hand and ran up the stairs. He was gone. I searched around the ground floor in a panic. Steve stood in front of the open door, staring into the darkness. It was then I noticed all the street and house lights were dark. I walked towards Steve. Outside stood Donna and the other hostages. Gabriel among them. I took Steve's hand again to walk outside. There were so many of us. The family I never had but wanted, united. All our souls on show, our freakish nature exposed.

"Come, daughter. The cleansing has begun and everyone like those who tried to harm you will meet their end. Only the ones with a soul will survive. We are many and you're not alone. We are the Legion to stamp out the hate."

★   ★   ★

Not only am I a bastard freak of nature, but I am also a killer of fascist pigs. It's something I can live with. Spencer Richardson was arrested and held without bail for drug trafficking, false imprisonment, money laundering. The best part was it was revealed he had been doing business with the cartels in South America and heroin operations in Afghanistan. All his white supremacist street cred down the motherfucking toilet. The true nature of his cause was revealed for all to see. His hideousness. The kind there is no room for and will be fucked out of existence.

We were not alone. I lay next to Steve, basking in the delight of release and pleasure, when the small knitting between my breasts opened. It's small; she's in the center of a petaled sticky membrane like a rose bud. She's coming back, re-growing. I've decided to name her Rose.

My phone vibrated.

Donna sent me a message. *You need to watch the TV. Any station. Hurry.*

We all sat up and I turned on the TV.

"These are scenes from around the world. Some say it's the end, as this has the potential to cause a global catastrophic event. Volcanoes around the world are erupting. But that's not all. This footage was shot in Mexico at Popocatepetl. The smoke from the volcano appears to meet thunderclouds in the sky. It also appears as if things are crawling from the ash. This is all we could see before the helicopter crashed."

Billows of gray smoke chimneyed out of the volcano. Lightning met the ground below soot-colored thunderclouds. The rumbling before the footage shut off sent chills across my body. Next to me, Steve grabbed my hand and squeezed. There, emerging from ash, were the faint outlines of shapes that could be humans scrambling across the Earth. My chest gurgled. I rubbed the red fault line on my chin before glancing at Steve. Wet streaks, tears of joy from the long-awaited reckoning, streamed down his face.

THE FINAL PORN STAR

1

Dennis stared at the large oak tree in disbelief and terror. Virginia, his beautiful Rottweiler, had refused to leave the back porch and stood whimpering by the sliding door. Now he knew why. His stomach gurgled as it flopped around like a clogged sink of dirty dishwater. The combined acid of juice and coffee percolated to a sudden stabbing sensation of heartburn. Breakfast soured until he bowled over and vomited into a pile of macerated fur. The sight of the vomit and the eviscerated animal caused him to heave again before he ran to call the police. With his hand on the door handle, he glanced back.

It looked like a Christmas tree decorated with meat that swayed in the breeze and glistened in the morning sunlight. Viscera dripped blood as it dangled from broken branches. Smaller branches had fallen to the ground where the goat and chicken carcasses lay cracked open like crushed cicada shells. How the hell, *who* the hell, would do such a thing? He heard absolutely nothing in the night. Now in his forties, he regularly got out of bed to relieve himself. Dennis wiped the saliva and dribbling vomit from his mouth with the back of his hand. He couldn't stop questioning what he was seeing. What kind of animal did this? How did it get to the top of the tree like that? It must have been big enough to topple some hefty branches that could have been twigs with the way they lay splintered. That only happened during storms. What terrified him even more was the thought it might be back, and not satisfied with half a dozen goats and chickens. He would sleep with his shotgun beneath his bed, double-check all the windows and doors were locked. Virginia would sleep at the foot of his bed, just in case.

★   ★   ★

"They really went cheap on this set. I mean, where *are* we?" Chase leaned closer to the car window, squinting in the midday summer sun.

"Beats me," I said. "I haven't been back to Texas in ages. Maybe it's in the middle of nowhere because it's *that* big. The photos looked great. Massive pool, jacuzzi cabin, bathtubs with jets that can fit four."

Chase readjusted the pillow between the door and his head. "I don't know. Looks creepy out here. Why did it have to be Texas? The longer we drive, the fewer signs of civilization I see. Feels like I'm walking into a slasher film instead of a porno." He lifted his phone to my face as he said this.

"Give it a chance; this is where I'm from. I only said yes because this is my final film and I wanted it to be in Texas since I'm moving here in a few months. It needs to be authentic. After all these years I'm out for good...and why the fuck you filming me?"

He stopped the video and smiled. "Because...and this was supposed to be a surprise, I'll be documenting the entire weekend. This is a big moment! I want to do something like *The Annabelle Chong Story*. Maybe submit it to a few film festivals. It'll be great. I promise. Just go with it!" He pressed his head into the pillow and closed his eyes.

I looked out my window to watch the countryside pass from utility pole to utility pole, as we headed to a ranch for my final pornographic film, *Vaquera*. It would be a nod to one of my first, *Rodeo*.

There is nothing great about me, or this strange journey of mine to warrant a story. Yes, it was a huge moment personally and professionally. I was through with porn, and it couldn't have happened at a better time. Once the video stores closed, and porn moved to the internet, it had been a slow decline for being a real star in porn. Anyone could create a video on their phone and call it porn. Now you had to worry about social media presence, giving the audience a deeper look into your insides while companies cut deeper into what you could make per scene. I felt too old for that shit. I did nothing interesting enough for Instagram or Facebook. Plus, my daughter just turned twelve and was desperate to join social media like her friends. I try to keep as low a profile online as possible for her sake, but it would be only a matter of time before she found me. And now Chase's big documentary bomb.

With one foot out the door, I managed to negotiate just me and one guy with the most basic of crews. I had to take a pay cut on this last film because I was eager to have my contract with Diamond films over and done with. Don't get me wrong, it was a lucrative contract, but it was time for another reinvention. I'd recently received my certification in high school career counseling with a contract with a school district in a tough neighborhood that didn't bat an eye at my change of work. I had enough saved in the bank to work in a profession that allowed me to give back to girls who came from places like I did. A place my daughter would never know. I only graduated from college at twenty-eight when I could pay my tuition in full every semester. No living in debt like my twenties. Throughout my career I directed, did makeup, sourced costumes, and did a bit of set scouting. I experienced every facet of porn since I was twenty. In two days, I would be forty. Still looked good too, with my brown skin hiding most of my wrinkles. Not a single injection to my lips, which were naturally full, and only the spot of Botox. Otherwise I was still in decent mid-life shape, avoiding the traps of hard partying and booze.

I guess my daughter helped curtail that. And before you ask, yes, I know the father. He's the stable, level-headed, boring-as-shit lawyer for Diamond Films. But nice guys are just that – nice. Then again you can't be that nice if you're married and fucking around with a porn star only to knock her up a few months later. He didn't have to be involved in my daughter's life; however, he chose to be present. I take the previous statement back. He is a good guy. We were never in love, just each other's lapse in judgment to distract us from the relationships that lacked the excitement of something new. He was also unfazed by my career because he worked in the adult entertainment industry.

I didn't think having a child was in my future. An entire layer of my cervix had to be removed to prevent cancerous cells from spreading in my early twenties. It was the final stop before cancer became life-threatening, but up to that point, I didn't have health insurance. I received all my birth control from Planned Parenthood, including my very sporadic pap smears. When you're young, you don't think anything out of the ordinary will happen to you. My high-priced private gynecologist made it very clear that carrying a child to term might require suturing my cervix. I also would be checked every six months to make sure the cancerous cells didn't return.

That was how I got into different roles in porn. I didn't want to be fucking with my baby inside of me, despite the offers with numerous zeros at the end. All I wanted to do was eat and fart in front of the television. Not really sexy. That's the kind of thing people are escaping from when they watch porn. I'm sure there are people with queff fetishes out there, but I didn't want to be part of that movement.

"Dammit!"

I forgot my reverie and whipped my head towards Chase. "What now?"

Chase made a big deal out of everything. That was what made

him a great director and a magician with the camera. His attention to detail and stomping until it was done right were the hallmarks of all his projects. Not a single ingrown hair went unnoticed by his hawk eye. Everything appeared softer when he was done lurking over some poor editor's shoulder. He ventured into porn right out of film school because when you're broke as a joke with defaulted student loans, you go where the paycheck is.

"Well, I hoped to do a whole Instagram Live thing for Diamond Films in honor of your final film. No service. Let's hope there's Wi-Fi. Everything I film will be automatically sent to my cloud in case it's sketchy."

I knew there was no fighting this documentary, so I'd play along. Maybe this would be a way to explain it all to my daughter when she was old enough to understand that all the opportunities afforded her had a cost. Big or small, life has a price tag.

We pulled off the highway, which was mostly semis barreling past, to a small road fit for two-way traffic. Nothing but fields, more utility poles, gas stations, then the occasional oil pump humping the earth for all it was worth, sucking out its moisture without mercy. There was supposed to be a diner out here attached to a truck stop famous for its barbeque. I'd have to hit it up on our way out. God, I looked forward to real Mexican food and barbeque.

The radio played Stevie Ray Vaughn's 'Little Wing'. I didn't mind but didn't want it turned up louder. I wanted to enjoy the rest of the ride in peace. This was miles from my twenty-year-old self, who walked the streets of Philadelphia hoping someone had dropped any amount of cash on the ground. I actively searched for accidental money. My mind was always plagued with what classes I might have to drop because I couldn't afford the books.

Not much stood between me and the homeless on the street. If I was hungry there were numbers I could call for dates, but fuck if I wanted to do that. I'd go home to my studio apartment and look for whatever I could spare to sell at Buffalo Exchange for cash. In college at least you could sign up for skin tests for cash in the science department. But all hope, in the big or small things, is nothing but a wet dream, an automatic response we have to life. It's better to wake up and find someone to fuck. And sometimes good luck finding that. You get more bad lays than good ones. I suppose that's why I answered that ad in the first place. I was already getting fucked by life, might as well get paid for it. Financially I was better off quitting school and doing film. After four years alone, the debt I would face kept me up at night as I stared at my computer screen in a small efficiency with crumbling, asbestos-filled walls.

We took another turn to a dirt road for half an hour. The continual bumping around made my new breasts ache. As much as I loved my new tits, they weren't practical by any means. I needed the extra filler after my child sucked everything out every few hours from breastfeeding. She was worth it.

Neither of us had a signal still. We were officially nowhere and stranded in a dead zone.

"Woman, this place better be phenomenal. You know what kind of roads are this bumpy? Roads that lead to nightmares!" Chase opened his eyes and pulled out his vaper. Once the THC hit his bloodstream, all would be good again. He took in a long drag before offering it to me. I shook my head.

"Chase, did you see how much booze I bought? There's enough champagne to poison us all. You know I like to smoke in the day, but it just puts me to sleep. I'll sip on wine, like a lady."

"Yes, I did see. It was noted because it's champagne and not just sparkling wine. I'm telling you now, don't go drinking too much tonight. You'll have a hella lot of close-ups between the documentary *and* the sex. Think *Deep Throat*, but good."

I pressed an elbow in his ribs, causing him to jump and bump me with his shoulder playfully. Even at my age, I was hotter than Linda Lovelace.

Tonight, we would sit in the hot tub strewn with multicolored lights with a disco ball attached to the ceiling. Tomorrow we filmed the first scene – solo sex in an outdoor shower room. Easy peasy. Secretly I hoped this would be the one that would land me an AVN award. Hell, I better at least be in the running for a lifetime achievement or something. Or maybe Chase was right and the story about the Final Porn Star would be the darling of the indie film festivals.

A wooden fence surrounded the property, which was neither luxurious nor modern. It was tired like me, the aging porn star.

The roof sagged from shingles that screamed to be replaced. The wraparound porch needed sanding and re-varnishing. There were no flower beds or flowering bushes, just cactus and agave plants sporadically growing in the yard. A cluster of palm trees grew to the right. At least the owners tried. It fit perfectly to the storyline of a beautiful lonely widow on a ranch in need of a hand. Pun intended.

A white Hummer sat parked in the front, which could only mean one thing: Randy arrived early. The noise from the dirt road must have alerted him to our presence because Randy walked out the door waving. That made two aging porn stars. Randy and I had been friends for years, and the reason I asked him to be my last was he was one of my first. I felt comfortable enough with him to tell him if something didn't feel right or his breath stank. We were the top-selling non-white stars for Diamond Films. At least we used to be before all these porn websites. There was now something for everyone with a quick scroll and click. Have you seen the categories section on those sites? Back then I did strip club tours to promote my films, conferences, signing video cases and t-shirts. Cover of *Playboy* and first Latina centerfold in *Hustler* magazine. A time long gone. A mythical creature, The Porn Star. Not some rich socialite taping herself in a mansion for shits and likes.

Randy wore a tight t-shirt and fitted skinny jeans, the kind all the young hip guys were wearing, and I despised like bras or thongs. Maybe it's my generation but I much prefer a man in baggy jeans that require a belt, grunge style. In fact, add a chain to the wallet for fun. Band or film t-shirt sloppily half tucked in. That or a tailored bespoke suit matched with Italian shoes and a French designer tie. He clamored down four stairs in flip flops, his smile as wide as his square jaw.

"How the hell are you?"

"I'm good! Long drive but we are here. Finally. When did you arrive?"

"About an hour ago. And I had time to go over this script." He took off his Gucci sunglasses that matched his Gucci logo-printed flip flops, giving me a jovial dissatisfied look. "No anal?"

I threw my head back and laughed. I knew he would rib me for that. My first anal film was with Randy and you would have thought I was studying for an exam by the way I grilled him about the scene.

The bag filled with sex toys and makeup was slipping of my shoulder. I hoisted it back up. "No anal. I don't want to spend the next few days expelling wet gas into my pretty panties or clenching in pain to shit. Panty liners were not made for the days post anal sex."

See, we were good enough pals that I could be honest about the reality of dirty taboo sex. A loose anus is not a happy one.

He raised his palms in surrender. "Hey, it's your show and your retirement. I have an anal film in a few months so I'm good. I just think it's a little suspicious you wrote in a massage scene." He gave me a playful wink.

Randy's fallback job was massage therapist. He knew he couldn't do porn forever. Who wants to? From what I heard he was damn good. Plus, massage porn is hot.

"I need a drink." I walked past him to check out the house. Chase waved him over to help unload the boxes of booze and extra luggage.

This was a ranch in every cliché sense. Antlers and pastoral paintings depicting farm life decorated the walls. A large fireplace, the location of one of the scenes, sat like a dark open mouth. Next to the fireplace was a landline phone that looked like it hadn't been used in years. Its white plastic casing was yellowed from age. Next to that was a black router with a blue sticky note reinforced with tape. The edges curled and showed specks of dust and fingerprints. *Wi-Fi out of order and no TV. Sorry!* Decks of UNO and playing cards sat next to the not-so-subtle note. Chase would not be happy. Hope his cloud worked.

A young woman half my age would be taking care of the sound. She was an all-American type with blonde hair and brown eyes and not a single crease between her eyebrows. I think she was Randy's new girlfriend. She sat on the sofa inspecting the boom. It felt odd to be filming in front of my co-star's latest squeeze, but I hoped being in the business eased her worry and reassured her we had zero interest in each other. Randy is the one who introduced me to my baby's daddy. We practically grew up together. Before our first film together he took me out for ice cream after seeing how nervous I was in the Diamond Film office. My hands shook with the contract in hand, the paper heavy with my guilt and nerves. Was I really going to do this? But I was desperate. Desperate with school debt and exhaustion. Over double scoops he explained the contract to me and reassured me God wouldn't smite me down when it was finished.

I sat next to her, dropping the heavy bag. "Hi, I'm—"

She put her equipment down and grabbed her phone that lay next to her. "I know exactly who you are. Thalia Sanchez."

I didn't want a confrontation and held my breath with a smile. "Oh. I just want to say—"

"Can I please have a selfie? I'm a huge fan. What you've done to elevate porn, sex work! Your sex toys for the homeless drive was epic. I can't believe how much you raised for charity. When Chase said we were making a documentary while filming you fuck...wow. I said I would do it for free! And to film most of it for Instagram...genius."

I felt a little self-conscious and a little old. "You don't mind Randy being my co-star?"

"Ha! Absolutely not. This is business. And it's not *that* sexy when filming."

I wasn't expecting that. She was right. Filming porn is not hot; the talent is in making it *look* hot. The fantasy. The things you want, but don't do with a house full of screaming kids and a partner you've fucked so many times every mole on their chest and hair on their thighs is memorized. And if you have no desire to be unfaithful, it can be a release from the pressure of monogamy. And monogamy can be such a damn drag. That's why I'm still single. Men also change their mind very quick when you tell them you are in porn, or any type of sex work. The exciting fascination sours eventually and pillow talk or words of love become a mouthful of sharpened teeth.

"You want to go check out the rest of the house? You need to see where the first scene will be filmed. It's really rustic, but romantic." Laura was all right. She seemed open-minded and kind. Nothing mattered except making it to the end of the weekend and finishing this film.

"Yeah, let's go."

The hot tub cabin and outdoor shower were surrounded by various species of palm trees of different heights and girths. The larger ones, with thickly ringed trunks, were bright on top with the bottom palms brown and brittle, hanging limply in ugly strings that looked like wrinkled hands belonging to a bruja. When I was growing up in San Antonio, our neighbors had a large palm in their yard. After dark I remember looking at it through the window, hoping la Lechuza wasn't there listening to my baby sister crying for a bottle, or me begging my mother to stay up later to watch a horror film.

The less-threatening ones, short and squat palms, gave the cabin a little privacy by partially blocking the windows. We walked to the side of the cabin to inspect the outdoor shower. I turned the handle to check the water pressure from a large flat spout made to give the sensation of falling rainwater. Cold then hot water spurted down on a wooden slatted floor that covered the drain. Cobwebs stuck to the corners with fat spiders lying in wait for some unsuspecting insect. I'd have to come out and clean that up before shooting. Chase would have a fit if I screamed mid filming from a spider landing in my hair or on my tits.

We walked back to the house for a drink to discuss the plan for the next few days with the schedule and budget as tight as latex. A new guy, mid to late twenties, but cute with dark brown hair falling to one side mid cheek, unpacked food from brown grocery bags in the kitchen. Poor kid would be doing all the grunt work. I motioned for Laura to follow me to the hallway.

"Hey, Laura. What's the deal with him?"

"His name is Blake. He's from the same film school as Chase. We met him at the airport and drove him down. Nice guy, never been on a film set like this before. Chase said he would be a cheap pair of extra hands."

Chase had failed to mention this. Typical Chase, always in charge. I would try to ignore the guy's boner once the filming started because if this was his first rodeo….

We stepped back into the living-room with Chase and Randy back from unloading the car and pouring everyone champagne in mismatched coffee mugs to toast the occasion. Chase had his phone out, filming the inside of the house, including the taxidermy heads surrounding the fireplace. Their glass eyes followed lifelessly.

"I wish this could be a haunted house porno. Look at this creepy shit. Who owns this again?" Chase asked. The camera swung in my direction.

"Your mama, Chase. Now stop the filming and drink with me."

2

That night, we feasted on hot dogs, bags of every potato chip fathomable, and a pre-made plastic bowl of salad. Like I said, I wanted to enjoy my last film, so I catered it the way I wanted. The five of us left the kitchen a mess and ventured to the hot tub cabin about sixty feet away. Blake carried a handful of Coronas in a bag and three bottles of champagne we would drink out of mugs.

In the darkness the pool glowed blue with steam rising from the surface. Besides the porch light and the pool, there were no other sources of light or properties that could be seen. The main road was too far to hear or see passing cars. Only visitors venturing to this home would drive down the dirt road. As far as we knew, no one else should show up.

Chase brought his portable speaker and used Blake's phone for music. He attached his phone to a selfie stick and pressed record.

"Lifestyle of the horny and famous here. Say hello to *the* final porn star." He switched the view on the phone then pointed to me.

"Hey y'all. It's me. We're having a blast making a great film for your enjoyment. My last one. Cheers!" I lifted my cup and took a long gulp.

Chase rolled his eyes. He probably expected me to flash the camera or do something outrageous. Old bitches like me do not do tricks. Show-pony days are done. I had slipped into being a middle-aged bore, not exactly going to command a huge audience any longer.

"Baby, I expect more enthusiasm tomorrow."

"Chase, you know you get the good stuff when you need it. Frankly, I'm tired. You'll understand when you're my age."

We drank and sang off-tune for hours, Randy and I recounting the good ol' days. I would miss the people I met in this industry, at least the ones I stayed in touch with. Entertainers came and went with the seasons and the reasons for staying in porn change too. The night spiraled into Randy and Laura making out in one corner of the hot tub, with me, Chase and Blake making small talk. Blake appeared more attractive hour by hour. Like that moody protégé of the evil emperor in the new *Star Wars* films. My daughter and I both had a slight crush on him. Blake tried not to look my way, our eyes meeting then pulling away back to our drinks.

"We're retiring for the evening," said Laura with heavy eyelids, dragging Randy out of the hot tub.

"Yeah, I'm done." Chase stood to leave. Blake looked at me like he wanted me to invite him to stay, but I remained silent.

"I'll join you," Blake said in a disappointed tone.

When everyone left, I let my body sink into the seat with the jets hitting my feet, massaging them. The booze elevated my temperature, making the water and room feel sweltering, but I was relaxed, high on the occasion and the alcohol. The room spun a little with the lights bouncing off the disco ball, purple and red shadows, like a makeup palette swirling above my head. I wasn't sure if I, or the room, was rotating.

I felt bad for the boys with all their student loan debt. For the first two years of college before I dropped out, I had to have this stupid meal plan, but with two jobs plus my class schedule there was no time to use the damn cafeteria. I survived on $2.50 steamed rice with tofu and broccoli topped with chili sauce from the campus food cart. If I wanted to splurge, a greasy chicken cheesesteak. I had to forge insurance papers because you had to have health insurance to be in school. My folks didn't earn enough to help so I was on my own.

To make ends meet I worked in a strip club as a shot girl. I sat under the lights, just like the ones in the hot tub cabin, in a bikini top and booty shorts with two heavy bottles at my waist like a gunslinger ready to get suckers blind drunk. But selling booze isn't the same as selling tits and ass. Same story for the massage girls. I didn't want to dance because those hours are killer. No way I could study and work the pole enough to make what I needed. Something would suffer, most probably my schoolwork. I had no assets but my body. My body and my desire for something, anything. Good girls don't always get good things or get paid.

And who made up the fucking rules anyway?

A scratch at the base of the cabin behind me jolted my senses back to life. I slid up, thinking I would see Chase's face between the palm fronds in one of the foggy windows with his phone or the camera pointed in my direction. Maybe Blake lurking.

Not a single human sound. No Chase or Blake. I turned back. The scratch seemed to drag against the base of the cabin, then became almost a digging sound. I sobered in my fear. I left the hot tub to turn off the disco ball's disorientating movement and color. My heart raced from the alcohol and heat before; now the palpitations threatened to break through bone. It had to be an animal, I told myself. I pressed the off button on the hot tub control panel as the water continued to bubble loudly. Nothing.

Still dripping wet, I grabbed my robe draped over a folding chair, then tucked my flip flops in the pocket because I could run faster without them.

It wasn't more than a one-minute walk from the cabin that housed the hot tub to the main house, but I didn't want to leave. The steam continued to fog the windows, making it impossible to see anything. I shouldn't have been scared; it wasn't like I was alone. The land was flat with very little to hide behind. Still, an unease crept over me. Slowly I opened the door. The coolness of the night air felt good. My mind felt more alert without the heat.

I looked to my left, swearing the palm moved despite there not being enough breeze to flip a leaf. I couldn't imagine what would be up at those heights. I didn't want to know. I dismissed it and ran hard for the house. The flagstone path and dirt hurt the soles of my feet. The screen and front door remained unlocked. Once inside I locked both and placed a dining chair in front. At least if someone broke in, we would hear them fall over this small obstruction. It wasn't much, just a little peace of mind. My heart still pounded. I walked to the window and peered out. Nothing but the calm water of the illuminated pool.

★   ★   ★

I woke up to the sound of Chase and Blake checking on the equipment, then the clanging of dishes in the kitchen. I did my own makeup as I had for the last few years – natural with a bright lip. The mark I would leave on this world was sticky cherry red.

I wrapped my nude body in my thick white robe to keep me warm from the freshness of the morning. Chase had a mug of filter coffee waiting for me when I walked into the kitchen.

"Morning. You want to have a little look with me? Need to check the light."

"I do. There are a few cobwebs in the shower that need to be wiped away. I'm ready to start this."

"Be sure to make it cute for the 'gram."

I rolled my eyes at him. We took our mugs before heading to the door.

"Chase, did you hear any noises last night?"

"Their fucking? How could I not? Randy says he lasts longer if he gets a good shagging before a film. I think I heard them both scream 'I love you.'"

I gave him a serious look as he stopped to open the screen door. "No. I heard scratching and screeching."

"Wait, babe," he said. "Let me turn this on." He flipped on his phone with one hand. "Okay. Let's go."

We walked onto the porch and down the three steps.

"Chase, as I was about to say, she was not scree—"

We both stopped mid-tracks at the foot of the porch. My mug quaked in my hands. A dead, no, dismembered and half-eaten coyote lay next to the hot tub cabin. I recollected the scratching from the previous night. But I looked in that direction and saw nothing. Deep slices streaked the trunk of the palm and broken palm leaves lay scattered around the hot tub. I couldn't remember if they were there before. But I noticed now.

"Holy shit! What the fuck? What the gross fuck!" Chase's phone recorded the gruesome scene. Without getting closer, he zoomed in on the carnage before turning the phone off and placing it into his back pocket. He turned and power-walked back to the house. The screen door banged loudly as he rushed in. I followed behind, not wanting to be near the torn carcass alone.

"Guys, we have a code red. Clean up on aisle four! There's a dead animal like roadkill outside, except there's no road or vehicle."

Randy stopped chewing half a piece of toast smothered in red jam. "Dude, I'm eating breakfast. What are you going on about?"

Chase pulled out his phone. "Fuck! Does anyone have a signal?"

We all looked at each other before glancing at ours. Not a single one of us had any bars to reach civilization. I didn't want this disruption to derail the film.

"Yo, Blake. You and I are on dead animal duty. Find some trash bags. Laura, clean out the shower of all the spiderwebs. Chase and Randy, find a place we can store the dead animal. I really don't want to smell it or see other animals digging through it. We'll have to email the owners when we get on the main road again."

I had to fight hard as hell not to puke as I shoveled the coyote remains into the bag. Flies swarmed greedily around me and my shovel. Blake and I took short breaks looking the other way while gagging on our saliva, our noses and mouths covered by spare bandanas I brought for my costumes. All I could think of was how would I make the solo shower scene convincing after this? I hated faking my solo scenes; they were the easiest and most enjoyable. I had to relax, think of anything besides death.

After an hour of clean-up, I ran in to scrub my hands despite wearing dishwashing gloves the entire time. What was out there last night? After this scene I would tell everyone what I heard. First, a shot of tequila to calm my nerves. I couldn't care less the time of day. Never had I felt this rattled before. Randy sat in the living room reading a book while the others milled outside, ready to shoot.

"Enjoy!" Randy shouted without breaking away from his page as I passed. The walk to the shower gave me goose bumps despite the temperature already being warmer, without a cloud to disrupt the May sunshine. Something in the pit of my stomach told me we should leave this place. The deep scratches on the palm caused another surge of panic as I passed the trees.

"Looking fly as hell, Ma." Chase held the camera while Blake recorded the scene with Chase's phone. However, he wasn't filming us. He focused on the damage to the tree.

I took the robe off and stepped into the shower. The Texas sky warmed my skin and suddenly the heat of the tequila burned through my anxiety. I was ready for a killer solo sex scene.

3

Dennis lay in bed with the shotgun next to him. The police officer who'd been sent out had found the scene as physically upsetting as Dennis and nearly vomited at the smell. Virginia refused to leave the house. She ate only a few bites of her meal before pacing around the kitchen.

Every house noise made him dart his eyes and hold his breath. Typically, he would have one beer with a sleeping pill, but not tonight. The officer had no idea and no other reports of this happening. He bagged a few samples and took photos then asked Dennis if he had any problems with anyone. Did he know any teens who would want to prank him?

Dennis felt like he was being questioned like an assailant. He said he would clean up the mess himself. It took all day, no lunch and multiple breaks, but he got it done using a ladder, broom and leaf blower. His back ached and twitched from digging a large hole in the ground to dump it all in.

He wished Elena was here. It had been a year since her passing, and nothing could make it better. The kids were gone and only Virginia was here to keep him company. He thought he should try a dating website because porn just didn't cut it anymore when he had an urge. Dennis missed having someone to talk to.

As his eyes began to grow heavy, Virginia bumped his hand and whined. Dennis couldn't tell if he was awake or asleep.

A crash of glass and metal. It wasn't a dream. Virginia barked loudly in his ear. He opened his eyes and saw the hulking frame in the door, but it was no man. Virginia growled low with a viciousness he had never heard from her before. The dark silhouette screeched like chainsaw on metal. He jolted up to grab the shotgun but the thing smelling like the flesh rotting in the tree lunged forward. He could feel his fingertips just brush Virginia as she leaped towards the intruder.

★　　★　　★

With the first scene over later than we anticipated due to the cleanup, we piled into the house to go over my scenes with Randy. Next, we prepared the master bedroom massage scene. A giant tiger skin comforter was spread across the bed. More distasteful taxidermy and antlers decorated the walls.

"Hey, Chase, should we take these things down?"

"Absolutely not! It's those details that'll take this to cult status. Sooo fucking creepy! Dead animals watching you fuck. We could not have staged this better. Honest to God, this will be the best film I've shot to date."

I would wear nothing – again – for the massage scene and Randy would be in just a pair of tight Wranglers. Warmed oil sat in a small glass pitcher on the side table. I lay on my belly, trying to relax, yet still felt on edge. My mind couldn't focus on any one thing, let alone sex. The warmth of the oil hitting the small of my back caused me to jump.

"Cut!" shouted Chase. "You all right? Need a drink? A puff on my vape?"

Randy leaned to my ear. "You need a minute?"

"No, I'm all right. I'll put my old acting classes to work."

I took a deep breath and thought of the first vacation I went on with my ex to Egypt. We had planned to go scuba diving, my first time, but it was the spring when a spate of shark attacks closed the beaches. We up ended staying in the room having nonstop sex and ordering in. Before I knew it, I was smiling as Randy began pressing his fingers into my back and ass.

*   *   *

None of us wanted to be near the bloodstained grass outside, which still seemed fresh with flies and gnats hovering over the lawn. The pool and hot tub lost all appeal. The smell of death, and perhaps of pieces we didn't find that were beginning to rot, got worse as the day wore on. It hung in the air and surrounded the ranch like the setting sun across the expansive Texas sky.

We stayed in, switching on all of the outdoor lights. Instead of meat, I made loaded nachos, corn on the cob, and a spread of Little Debbie cakes as a side. And a lot of booze. With no internet and no cable TV, we sat around the coffee table in the front room in our pajamas and sweatpants.

"So, what kind of animal you think it was? I mean, coyotes are pretty fierce," said Laura as she linked her arm with Randy's. They both wore matching loose, plaid cotton trousers and ribbed t-shirts.

"Maybe it was a monster?" We all turned to Blake, who inhaled from Chase's vaper.

"And what do you know of monsters?" I asked.

"You're Mexican. You know. We grew up with all those stories."

Yeah, I did know, and it scared me to death. I never told my daughter the stories I heard as a child. Discipline growing up was the threat of a chankla across your ass, or some supernatural creature ready to take you away. God, how parenting had changed.

Before I could speak, Chase chimed in. "Okay. Nope. We are not telling ghost stories on a night like this. I'm already freaked out."

Randy leaned closer into Laura. "I want to hear your stories," he said to me. "What else are we going to do? We got to save the good stuff for tomorrow."

"You wanna go first, or me?" I asked Blake.

Blake tipped a shot of Jim Beam into a glass before downing it. "You. I need a little more of this first."

"The first story I actually experienced on my tenth birthday. Well, you all know I'm from San Antonio, few hours from here. There's a portion of train tracks they say is haunted by children on a bus that got hit by a train after it stalled on the tracks. No survivors. Legend says you sprinkle baby powder on your rear window, park on the tracks, then put your car in neutral. Slowly you'll feel your car moving across to the safety of the road. Get out of your car and look at the baby-powdered window. You might see small handprints from the souls of the children pushing you to safety."

"The fuck. You did this at ten?"

"Yes, Randy, with my mother. I had to try it myself. And the car moved. My mother pulled to the side of the road after we rolled off the tracks and we both went to inspect the window."

The four watched me in silence, slack-jawed.

"I don't know if it was movement from the car or the wind, but some of the baby powder was gone. Wiped away."

"You, Blake? What's your story?"

Blake's knee bounced up and down. "I know I'm young, but

I have a kid. My then girlfriend, Dani, got pregnant when we were fifteen. At that time, there were no options for us, her. I was at her mom's house one night and my son, Jordan, would not stop crying. Dani wouldn't stop crying. We tried everything. Finally, after what seemed like hours, he fell asleep. Dani and I went to the back porch for a smoke. As we sat on the back porch, something scratched at the side of the house. We thought maybe a stray, so we looked closer because it was outside the baby's room. I was gonna kill anything that woke my son again. In the darkness, a large shape hunched over. The smell was a mix of shit and decay. I will never forget the smell. The only way I can describe what was scratching at the wall was a large claw beneath a robe, or I don't know. Dani's mama-bear instinct kicked in while I remained chicken shit. Boy, she screamed then grabbed the lighter from my hand. When it flicked on, she rushed towards it. The thing screeched. And I shit you not, it flew off. After that we ran into the house and lay in the dark close to the baby. The next morning, we looked at the window...." Blake took another drink followed by a suck on Chase's vaper. "The screen was completely tore up, and the glass was cut with deep grooves."

Chase grabbed his vaper back from Blake. "Did you say *screech*?"

I felt like I needed to lighten the atmosphere because I was starting to feel afraid. Part of me always harbored suspicions there had to be some kernel of truth to the legend. "Sounds like la Lechuza. One of the stories I heard growing up. Body of an owl and head of a witch. It's one of the many stories about creatures, like the chupacabra, we tell misbehaving kids."

"Well, Dani swears to this day it was la Lechuza. I try not to think about it. Until the other day."

None of us could tear our eyes from Blake. The silence was like that moment in a horror film where the killer raises their axe to strike.

Laura sat upright. "The fuck was that?"

We looked around, honing our ears to the faintest of sounds. There was a bump on the front door. A scratching and whimper. Randy inched to the edge of the sofa to get up, but I sat closer. I looked around for whatever I could use as a weapon. Randy stood at the same time as me and we both quietly crept towards the window next to the door. I assumed he thought his brawn could be used.

We'd closed the drapes earlier, unlike the previous night. Only moving the fabric as much as I needed to see, I looked out to the glowing pool. It remained undisturbed. Another scratch. I glanced down to see a large dog, a rottweiler. I yelped instinctively.

Randy lunged closer to the window, opening the curtain halfway. "Poor baby! Look at her. She's shivering. Look at the cut on her face and paw. Open the door. Quick."

I fumbled at the lock and the bolt. The dog rushed in, barking loudly. Blood seeped from one paw and a large gash slashed across her nose. Both ugly, probably painful, but she would be okay. Randy kneeled to inspect the wounds and calm her down.

I glanced outside once more before locking the door and placing a chair in front.

Blake bolted up at the sight of the dog pacing nervously yet accepting the affection from Randy and now Laura. "There's a first aid kit beneath the sink. I'll get it." He brought two hot dogs from the fridge and the kit. The dog hungrily ate the meat while Randy gingerly cleaned her scrapes. A tag dangled from her neck: *Virginia*. On the opposite side was an address we couldn't even look up because of the lack of service.

Laura looked like she was on the verge of tears and fear. "Why don't we give her a bath? She looks filthy. I don't think this dried stuff on her coat is her blood."

"Come on, baby girl. You're safe now."

Virginia looked at the door and barked once before standing to my side. I scratched her head and kneeled to face her. "It's okay, girl, go have a bath." I stood and walked towards Randy. She allowed herself to be led to one of the empty rooms with a spare bath.

Chase took a deep inhalation from his vaper. "Guys. I'm scared. Blake, are you shitting me with that story?"

Blake took out his wallet. "See, here's my son and his mom. I wouldn't make something up like that. Believe me, I'm just as freaked out as you. Seeing the damage to the tree outside brought it all back."

According to the clock in the kitchen, it was eleven p.m. "Why don't we call it a night?" Chase's eyelids sagged from the THC and were reddened with fear. Sleep was a good call, but there was something else on my mind.

"I was thinking we should finish taping tomorrow. Screw another scene and leave before dark. I don't want to stay another night. Fuck Diamond Films. I'll make sure you get your money. I just have a bad feeling about this."

Chase gave me a disappointed look. "I know what you mean. Why don't we all get some much-needed rest and talk about it tomorrow?"

For some reason, Virginia followed me into the bedroom after her bath even when Randy tried to tempt her with another hot dog to sleep with him and Laura. I didn't mind, as I didn't want to sleep alone. My thoughts turned to my daughter, who I missed more than ever. At first Virginia stood alert by the window with the blinds shut. We both watched the dark square in fear, waiting for the slightest noise. But I needed sleep. We had to shoot the majority of the sex scenes in the morning. I wanted to go. My eyes didn't leave Virginia until she lay down to rest. I wondered where she was from and what she saw before I drifted to sleep.

★   ★   ★

Virginia pulled out a mouthful of feathers before pain exploded across her nose.

"Fuck you! Run, Virginia! Don't come back!" screamed Dennis. Metal hit his nose with a loud crunch ringing in his ears. Hot breath blew his hair across his face and in his nose. Blood from his nostrils streamed into his mouth, which he had to open to breathe.

More cracking and screams as the thing settled on his thighs, crushing him. He looked to his night table at the photo of his deceased wife, Elena Cruz, hoping he would see her soon. He remembered the day she died and how much she loved reading to him because he wasn't a big reader unless it was the sports or weather page of the newspaper. He looked back at the bulbous eyes and black beak of the beast, remembering one particular story. It was a Mexican folktale they both laughed off. The tale looked at him with hungry malice. He sat back and allowed it to take him to his wife.

Virginia ran down the stairs and out the ripped-open door into the night. There was only one other place she remembered with the scent of her mother: an old ranch house.

★   ★   ★

The crack and boom were what woke us all up and caused Virginia to howl.

Chase looked refreshed from a full night of sleep despite his eyes being wide and hair stuck in the air. Then came the sound of rain pounding against the house. Part of me was relieved. We would all agree to pack it in and leave. Blake videoed the storm outside then turned the camera to us.

"It's fine. Everything is fine," Chase said. "We'll move the scenes inside. I just need time to think." He looked really distressed, more than I had ever seen him before, and we had known each other going on five years now.

"Why don't we just leave?" I asked. "We can make it up later."

"I can't, Thalia. I need the money. My family needs the money. My abuela is not doing well and should be in a nursing home, and not some crappy, dirty place. And I hoped this documentary could be a way out of porn for me too. And where are we going to go? We can't exactly check flight times."

My heart sank.

"Yeah, I don't want to leave either." Blake stood there, no longer filming.

"Dammit!" Chase screamed. He looked at his phone. "Still no signal or weather report."

I tried to calm him. "Look, storms in Texas come hard and fast. I'm sure it'll be over in an hour. We can make it after."

He looked at me with eyes as pleading as Virginia's. "Fine. We'll regroup and come up with another scene if it doesn't." He shuffled back to his room.

Laura went to the kitchen to start a pot of coffee and the rest of us went to our rooms to get ready. The rain continued to hammer down.

I brought toast and coffee to the creased leather sofa perpendicular to the fireplace in the living room. I could smell ammonia, strong enough it had to be coming from inside the house. None of the windows seemed to be open. I got up to look around to see if perhaps Virginia had relieved herself. Next to the fireplace, ash and dirt dusted the floor. I couldn't remember if it was there before. Did a bird find its way into the chimney, or had the storm disturbed something stuck inside? The closer to the fireplace I got, the stronger the smell. I was afraid to look. I kneeled and craned my neck up the dark chimney. Nothing but the disgusting stench. I wanted to leave. Too many strange coincidences.

"I know some of y'all will miss that ass. I know I will."

I turned to see Chase recording me with his phone. I couldn't smile, but at least he had regained his sense of composure.

"What are you doing there?" he asked.

"Chase, turn it off for a sec." The look on my face must have alarmed him because he stopped immediately, and kneeled next to me.

"Come closer. Do you smell that?"

He sniffed and scrunched his nose. "I mean this whole place is a bit off. Something got caught up there and died? I don't know. Make sure you ask for some money back."

"And look here. Ash and dirt. Do you remember this from yesterday?"

He looked around then back at the fireplace. "I know the other day was hella scary, but I think you might be overreacting a bit. The rain, you think?"

"I'm not overreacting. I think we should finish this and leave as soon as possible."

"Before we talk about breaking contract, let's see how far we get. I honestly think everything is fine. We have big ol' Virginia. I need this, Thalia."

Virginia padded in with Laura to take her outside. After Virginia finished her business, she ran back to my room to pace restlessly, leaving wet paw prints on the floor. What did she sense or see before she found us?

While we continued to wait out the storm with no end, we ate lunch silently.

The outdoor scene moved to an indoor scene with me in a white off-the-shoulder cotton nightgown that fell just below my ass cheeks. All I had to do was lean back on the bed and serve Randy with an all-you-can-eat buffet, then return the favor to him. After, a shower and costume change into my favorite white lace bodysuit with garters and stockings that had an opalescent shimmer to them. I chose white because I liked the way it contrasted with the color of my skin, and ever since I was a girl, I always had a thing for Madonna's video for 'Like a Virgin'. Over the stockings, brown ass and crotchless leather chaps buckled at the waist. And a holster for a sex toy. I might not have wanted anal sex, but it didn't mean the area was off limits.

I left my makeup simple but with a bold lip; this was a film set on a ranch, not a cabaret. I wanted that sense of telenovela beauty and drama. Windswept for the scenes outside, reminiscent of an old romance novel. Chase and I agreed it would be the kind of film a woman would want to watch to get off or share with a partner. If I wasn't bored and tired and past the age that men pay attention to women, I would have started my own ethical porn company. Yeah, you heard me right. One hundred percent non-exploitative sex for your viewing pleasure. Ages of performers verified, no trafficking. This film would be something like that. The more I thought about it, the more I liked the idea of all of this being documented to show how I've changed and how the porn industry has changed, considering I was a certified over-the-hill veteran.

"Remember, ladies and gents, this is not for your pleasure but theirs. I need to be able to see what's happening."

"Chase, we're old-head professionals. We know our angles. And it'll look like I'm loving every second of it. No offense, Randy."

"Everyone ready? Let's finish this!"

I tried not to worry or stare at the dead animal trophies hanging on the walls.

4

Blake stopped me in the hallway of the bedrooms. Randy had already headed into the shower after our scene and I needed to shower and change into my chaps outfit. I decided to pack to facilitate a quick getaway from the ranch.

"Hey, Thalia," Blake said. "I don't know if it's just me, but is there something kinda between us here?"

I gave him a blank expression. "It's just you, kid. This is business for me. Sorry to catch your feelings...or cock."

He looked down with a shy, boyish look, his long emo hair falling over one eye. I noticed he wore his swimming trunks. "You sure you want to go out there? I think it's best we stay in after dark."

"Well, I was hoping to spend time with you. Anyway, I think it's all good. No crying babies here except me. The marks on the house and tree freaked me out, but it's nothing."

I kissed him on the cheek. "Don't stay out too long, mijo. We have our last scene to shoot." Then I shot him a playful wink.

I watched him walk away, admiring his youthful body. I didn't like the idea of staying here another night or us not sticking together inside. Laura and Chase went over the footage taken so far while discussing editing ideas. After my shower, quick change and repacking my bag so I could zip it up and leave, I glanced at the time on my phone. Virginia lay sound asleep at the foot of my bed. The poor girl had been on tenterhooks since she arrived. Before joining the others, I closed the door firmly so she would not be disturbed. I walked out to the front room, hearing only three voices. No Blake. A feeling of panic gripped my stomach.

"Guys, I think we should check on Blake."

"Yeah, he's been out there a long time," said Laura.

I continued to stand there, feeling like an ass, not wanting to go out alone.

Laura must have noticed. "You want company?"

I nodded silently.

She looked at her phone again for service before tossing it back on the sofa. I assumed still nothing.

MESTIZA BLOOD • 191

I grabbed a knife from the block on the kitchen counter that would barely cut through a thick t-bone steak, but it made me feel safer anyway.

"Are you really that spooked, Thalia?" Laura frowned at the knife.

All I could do was nod again. Before we stepped out, Virginia began to bark at the door and whimper.

"Hey, girl, it's okay." Randy ran his hand the length of Virginia's body.

This reinforced my fear, but I had to check on Blake. We walked out the door to Virginia still barking. The mugginess of the day turning to night threatened to suffocate me as much as the stillness, like the very darkness held its breath and shut its eyes as to what lurked in this remote place. Mosquitos flocked to my bare skin, painfully taking their fill of my blood. From outside the hot tub cabin, the lights bounced on the revolving disco ball; the windows, fogged from the heat, made it impossible to see inside unless we opened the door.

It creaked open.

Blake's head bobbed in the water, which bubbled bright red. It ping-ponged against the sides of the hot tub. Laura and I both screamed. Footprints that smelled like a combination of manure, ammonia and mud surrounded the tub. But they were not human. They looked like something a bird would leave. At the corner, a hole had been dug beneath the cabin wall. The scratch marks reminded me of the gashes on the tree.

Laura stared at the dismembered body parts. "Oh my God. Oh my God. We're being hunted by some inbred country bumpkin!" She began to back towards the door, her entire body rigid from the terror.

The knife quaked in my hand. I grabbed her arm to pull her closer to me. "Shh. He could be out there, or it." I felt just as terror-stricken but knew I had to survive this.

The room was silent except for the bubbling water. Disco-ball shadows glittered across the room as it turned. With the light on,

I couldn't see outside. I turned around and switched off the ball. We both peered through the door, expecting to see the silhouette of a masked man holding a machete or a cleaver. It was then we heard a scream come from the house.

Laura looked at me, gripped in horror. "Randy!"

My heart tumbled and skipped. What the fuck were we going to do? We had no idea what was happening and no weapons. "We have to help him. Maybe there's something in the kitchen." All I had on me was a dull knife, a holstered dildo and soft rope, meant for teasing not killing. Phones didn't work.

"Where are Randy's car keys?" I asked.

Laura's eyes darted before she squeezed them shut as we continued to hear screams from inside the house. "Uh. Um. I think in our bedroom. I don't know; we haven't used the car since we arrived. Probably in our room."

The screams stopped. Laura's lips trembled; she shook her head. "Let's go," she said.

The light of the pool and the two lights in the house would have to illuminate our way. Neither of us had a plan except to get out alive.

I opened the door, expecting to hear a fight or screaming. Loud slurping and the crack of breaking bones filled the house. Virginia barked behind my door. I couldn't believe my eyes when I saw what was right in front of me in the hallway. I grabbed Laura's head and placed my hand over her mouth before she had a chance to scream. Her entire body trembled violently against me. It couldn't be. My brain thumped as hard as my heart. I knew what it was. You're told as children that la Lechuza waits in the dark. With the head of a witch and the body of an owl, it waits to steal wailing, misbehaving children.

This thing was neither small, nor a witch. But it did have the face of a human and the body of a feathered creature. La Lechuza crouched over Chase's body. Serrated teeth plucked at his heart, pulling at the tough muscle. Blood oozed from the wounds and splashed across the creature. Powerful clawed feet stomped on limbs to crush the bones beneath the skin. Whenever it chewed, its teeth clacked and grinded against each other. From the neck down, the body was all feathers. There were small domes where breasts should be, but no genitals I could see. Who knew what was beneath? It had spindly arms covered in feathers with a flap of skin that hung low at the bottom, like wings, but I couldn't imagine this thing flying, not at its size. It was impossible to tell the color of the creature because dried blood and dirt coated its body. The wings stopped at the wrists. Elongated fingers, bright red, capped with claws, picked the thickest morsels of flesh. As it swallowed, it tossed its head back; the gullet quivered to swallow, making a guttural sound. The back molars or whatever was inside that monster gnashed. It still did not notice us in its feast of flesh.

My gaze fixed upon my dead friend, split from the base of his skull to his anus. His vertebrae protruded with chunks of muscle missing. The torn flesh looked as if a wild animal had scavenged for garbage. If this was la Lechuza, eater of children and drinker of babies' blood, why here? We were all consenting adults getting fucked up and fucking. Then I remembered the location. We were not even an hour away from the border. My body shivered. I thought of my daughter in her lavender and rainbow bedroom full of books and toys. I thought of the other children without those luxuries. The cruelty of the government at the border. Was this thing drawn to the suffering here? My next thought was how could I survive or kill it. We had no guns. The largest blade in the house was a steak knife, which I held. All I had on me was a large vibrator with a massive head that had twenty-five vibration settings.

From the corner of my eye I could see the walk-in pantry door crack open. Randy's head poked out. He held his index finger to his lips. Laura waved her hand towards him to join us at the door. La Lechuza continued to eat. Randy opened the pantry just enough to fit through. With slow, cautious steps he made his way from the kitchen to us. I could feel the tension in Laura's body as she trembled against me. Just as he was about five feet from us, we heard a screech. It finished its meal yet wanted more. It was like nothing I had ever heard before. It rose to its full height. Randy was a big guy, but this was bigger. He turned towards the screeching creature.

"No!" screamed Laura.

Before the thing could pierce Randy through the heart with its claw, Laura got there first. The sharp point slashed across her head, taking off her crown of blonde locks. With its other claw it pierced her neck. She gave her life for him.

"Randy!" I yelled to get him to move before the thing got him too. It was too late. It swiped its other claw, ripping his head clean off his shoulders. The screech was now almost a fit of laughter. Before I could react, it thrust its head into my chest, the wind flying out of my mouth, causing me to choke and gasp for air. The left side of my chest exploded in pain with a sensation of deflation. My implant! The damn monster bird popped my tit. It lunged at me with one claw as I tried to recover my breath. Before I could tumble away the tip sliced through the leather of my chaps, and into my thigh. It poised to attack again.

The rope and the vibrator, still in the holsters at my side, and the knife in my hand were the only weapons at my disposal. I grabbed the vibrator with my free hand to use as a club. La Lechuza lunged at me again. I reacted by squeezing the vibrator, turning on its rapid circular movements and buzzing sound.

La Lechuza hissed at me in confusion. I lifted the knife to thrust into its body when it attacked. As it rushed at me with its claws outstretched I waved the vibrator, causing it to screech and swing its claws. I moved to its side. When it swept its wing and claws, I dove into its chest, plunging the knife into the spot where the wing met its body; no feathers, only a soft pinkish exposed skin that allowed it to extend its wings. Another deafening screech.

Big problem. The knife remained inside of the monster. La Lechuza stumbled and twisted, trying to remove it. I ran to my bedroom door to let Virginia out. She had been growling and barking hysterically and wasted no time running to the creature and sinking her jaws into its right leg. Her head shook violently between snarls. The creature buckled to the ground. I took this opportunity to put the vibrator down my bodysuit. The movement hurt but I needed it close to keep the creature distracted. I grabbed the rope and secured it around its neck, loop after loop. I tightened it as much as I could. La Lechuza continued to chomp at the air with jagged teeth as Virginia barked and bit with fury, the kind of rage that accompanies female vengeance. One hand held on to the rope as I ducked flapping wings and claws. With my free hand I grabbed the oversized vibrator from my bodysuit. The sound of the rotating head caused the creature to buck, its eyes rolling in erratic panic and confusion. It was scared.

I shoved it into its jaws. It gagged and sputtered. The last bite inadvertently turned the vibrator to a more vigorous twirling movement, causing it to lodge deeper into its throat. The creature's hands clawed at its face.

I grabbed the knife out of its body and rammed it into the side of the creature's neck. Black blood sprayed my face and body. The stench made me want to gag. This seemed to renew its anger as it continued to gurgle with the vibrator whirring in its gullet and the gash leaking blood. I had to finish the job. You always have to finish the job. Never, and I mean never, leave the killer without knowing for certain it is dead. Virginia barked, her mouth and teeth blackened and full of feathers.

I looked around in panic for anything else to kill the beast. The crate of champagne and alcohol. I grabbed the vodka and dumped it in its open mouth. Then a bottle of red with a screw top. It gurgled, unable to close its mouth with the vibrator opening its throat. I would drown the fucker in booze. I popped open a bottle of champagne and watched it fizz in the mouth filling with alcohol. The creature's neck bulged; its eyes rolled back. The wings flapped less the more I poured, until I couldn't fill its body any longer.

Virginia stopped barking, watching as she panted in morbid fascination as I did. There was only the sound of gurgling and buzzing. The chest of the creature no longer moved. I brought the open bottle of champagne to my mouth and took a long drink. My wounded chest and leg stung in a searing pain that made me want to collapse like a corpse. I noticed it now that the fight-or-flight adrenaline started to wear off. Another drink from the bottle to dull the pain. When I finished the bottle, I broke it against the fireplace. I used whatever strength I had left to press the broken bottle into the chest of the creature where the heart would be. Blood flooded out and I knew it was over.

My career, these friendships and la Lechuza.

What would be said about this night?

Suddenly, the sense of despair that I felt earlier returned. All I wanted was to see my daughter again, my bright child who would have choices her mother didn't have. She would always know I was proud of her. I didn't survive this long to give up now. I knew I should not be driving even after one drink, yet I had no choice. I would only go as far as I needed to get a signal. I went to Randy and Laura's bedroom, trying not to look at their bodies through my tears. What would I tell their families? The police? On the dresser were the keys to the Hummer. There was also a bottle of water, which I chugged.

I stepped over the carnage again, saying a prayer for my friends. Virginia followed behind and I was happy to have her there. As I walked out, two lights approached from down the road. I hobbled towards them and waved my hands. Virginia barked. It was the highway patrol. A man who looked about the same age as Blake stepped out and ran towards me. He must have been startled seeing a bloody woman in lingerie and dog covered in la Lechuza goo.

"Are you all right, miss?"

"My friends…."

"We got a strange call from a resident not too far from here who had a bad disturbance the other day. We've been patrolling the area and looking at all the properties. Why don't you get in the car and we'll get you somewhere safe. Is this your dog?"

Virginia stepped close to me and licked my hand.

"Yes, she is."

When we got a signal, I had just enough energy to text my daughter to tell her I loved her. There was a ringing tone. I looked at my phone, but nothing. It was coming from inside the holster. Before leaving the house, I grabbed everyone's phones from the kitchen counter for their families. The notification was from Chase's phone, indicating upload to the cloud was complete. I sat up. Everything that occurred had been filmed. Everyone would know la Lechuza, that monsters are real. I couldn't stop shaking. There I was, the final woman, the final porn star.

But I survived.

FLAME TREE PRESS
FICTION WITHOUT FRONTIERS
Award-Winning Authors & Original Voices

Flame Tree Press is the trade fiction imprint of Flame Tree Publishing, focusing on excellent writing in horror and the supernatural, crime and mystery, science fiction and fantasy. Our aim is to explore beyond the boundaries of the everyday, with tales from both award-winning authors and original voices.

•

Other titles available by V. Castro:
The Queen of the Cicadas

Other horror titles available include:
Snowball by Gregory Bastianelli
Thirteen Days by Sunset Beach by Ramsey Campbell
Think Yourself Lucky by Ramsey Campbell
The Hungry Moon by Ramsey Campbell
The Influence by Ramsey Campbell
The Haunting of Henderson Close by Catherine Cavendish
The Garden of Bewitchment by Catherine Cavendish
The House by the Cemetery by John Everson
The Devil's Equinox by John Everson
The Toy Thief by D.W. Gillespie
One By One by D.W. Gillespie
Black Wings by Megan Hart
The Playing Card Killer by Russell James
The Siren and the Specter by Jonathan Janz
The Sorrows by Jonathan Janz
Castle of Sorrows by Jonathan Janz
The Dark Game by Jonathan Janz
House of Skin by Jonathan Janz
Hearthstone Cottage by Frazer Lee
Those Who Came Before by J.H. Moncrieff
Stoker's Wilde by Steven Hopstaken & Melissa Prusi
Creature by Hunter Shea
Ghost Mine by Hunter Shea
Slash by Hunter Shea
The Mouth of the Dark by Tim Waggoner
They Kill by Tim Waggoner
The Forever House by Tim Waggoner

•

Join our mailing list for free short stories, new release details, news about our authors and special promotions:

flametreepress.com